# DARE TO FC

*The Dare Series 3*

## DIXIE LYNN DWYER
**Copyright © 2015**

# Chapter 1

"I don't know why you can't try to talk with him. He is your father, Adel," her mom Gladys told her over the phone. Adel took a deep breath and released it. She was at work. She didn't need this call today or any day for that matter. Why couldn't her mom understand how hurt Adel was?

"I have nothing to say to him. I really can't talk right now. I'm working."

"You wouldn't have to work if you were with Bentley."

Her mother's comments were so cruel and sliced through her heart like a very sharp knife. How could she say these things to her?

*Easy for you to say, but I for one will not marry or be with a man who isn't faithful.*

"I'm sorry, Mom, but I need to go."

She disconnected the call and then tossed the cell phone into her bag on the floor next to her chair. She lowered her head, rubbed her temples, and closed her eyes.

The instant headache was right on cue. It always followed a conversation like this one with her mom. Then came the images. Bentley Ross, her fiancé, had cheated on her. Not once. Not twice. Hell, not three times but too many to track and prove. Considering she had photographs and documented hotel room receipts with video surveillance, there was no way the lying weasel prick could get away with it. None of that concrete evidence mattered to the power-hungry business tycoon she was to call her father? No. When he chose Bentley and a business merger over his own daughter that was it for her. She practically growled with her teeth clenched. She took a deep breath and then exhaled. She was at work. She didn't need this aggravation.

"Adel?"

She heard the deep voice and looked up to see Leo and Hank, two of her bosses. She sat up straight, her head pounding, and forced a smile. "Good morning, Leo, Hank, can I get you some coffee?" she asked, getting up too quickly. She gripped the desk then felt the hand on her arm steadying her.

"Whoa, are you feeling okay?" Leo asked her.

"Oh yes. I just…I just got up too quickly. I'm fine. Really," she said, staring into Leo's dark blue eyes. The man was intense and his entire body, including his face, appeared chiseled from stone. Even in the dress pants and dress shirt she could tell how fit he was. She swallowed hard.

He reached out and caressed her cheek. The man was taller than most. His brothers were close at six foot three.

"You look a little flushed. Could you be coming down with something?" he asked, appearing concerned. She knew better. These men were hard, strict, demanding men that didn't show much thoughtfulness or concern. Fourteen months she worked for them and she still couldn't read them entirely. They were all business. It both aroused her and reminded her too much of the past.

"No. Just a headache."

"Well, be sure to take something. The last thing we need is for you to spread some sort of sickness or virus through the office. We've got a lot to work on," Hank stated, giving her the once-over then

# DARE TO FORGIVE

## *The Dare Series 3*

## Dixie Lynn Dwyer

**MENAGE EVERLASTING**

**Siren Publishing, Inc.**
**www.SirenPublishing.com**

**A SIREN PUBLISHING BOOK**
IMPRINT: Ménage Everlasting

DARE TO FORGIVE
Copyright © 2015 by Dixie Lynn Dwyer

ISBN: 978-1-63259-765-6

First Printing: August 2015

Cover design by Les Byerley
All art and logo copyright © 2015 by Siren Publishing, Inc.

Printed in the U.S.A.

**PUBLISHER**
Siren Publishing, Inc.
www.SirenPublishing.com

# DEDICATION

Dear readers,

Thank you for purchasing this legal copy of Dare to Forgive. May you enjoy Adel's story as she fights her own fears, reservations and anxiety from her past and those who had hurt her. She has a wall over her heart. A mental and physical block that keeps her from getting too close and even trusting people, especially men. It will take something powerful and pure to break down those walls and help her to trust again.

But she has such a big heart, and just wants to feel loved, that she risks everything to give the family that hurt her so badly a second chance in order to accept true love from three men that adore her. That chance nearly costs her her life.

Enjoy the story.

Happy reading.

Hugs!

~Dixie~

walking by. She felt contaminated as she pulled her bottom lip between her teeth and stared at her desk.

Leo had already released her arm. He touched her hand.

She looked at him.

"Don't mind him. You should know by now how grumpy he is in the morning. Plus we're working on a big contract. We'll need you to take some notes and do a few phone calls. Will you be okay in about ten minutes?" he asked, sounding concerned.

She was still bent over Hank's insulting comment about possibly spreading a virus through the office. Men were all the same. Maybe Leo was just being nice because he wanted something from her? By the way they always had plans and by the phone calls she had to forward to them, she'd say they were ladies' men.

"I'll be fine," she replied when she realized she was staring at him.

"Good, and if you don't have any ibuprofen to take, I have some in my top desk drawer."

"That's okay, I have my own. Thank you, Leo."

He winked at her, holding her gaze a moment too long, making her belly flutter with curiosity, but then he turned around and headed toward his office.

She needed the painkillers quick. With her head hurting this much she was bound to miss something one of them said in the meeting and then Hank would bite her head off. No thank you. She reached into her bag and grabbed the water bottle and the large bottle of ibuprofen. Staring at it a moment she realized it was getting low. This was a definite indication of how much the past and her mom's weekly phone calls were weighing their toll. *Maybe if I just forgive them and forget them, they'll leave me the hell alone?*

Now all she needed was a call from Bentley

\* \* \* \*

"Is she getting the ibuprofen?" Hank barked at Leo over the phone.

"Yes, but she's staring at the bottle. She looks so upset. Something is going on with her," Leo added, feeling very concerned. He wondered if she got a call from her mother. It seemed to him whenever Adel's mother called she hit that bottle for the painkillers, instantly getting a wicked headache. What would her mother say to her to get her so upset?

"It's none of our business. We have more important things to prepare for, like this potential project. Don't you realize how much money could be made from this construction project?" Hank asked, sounding very serious. Leo wondered when his brother would admit to his feelings for Adel. After all, he and Will were growing impatient and if they held out any longer they could potentially lose the chance they wanted.

She was perfect for them.

"I know exactly how much money we can make. I also know how many more workers will need to be hired and how much aggravation will go into a construction project this big. It's a three-year project with three phases of building," Leo said to Hank.

"That's not all. Don't forget about the community center that will need building, the schools from elementary up to high school, and even the shopping center. This is what we've been waiting for and our opportunity to snag it isn't going to be easy," Hank added.

"It isn't going to be easy and especially up against some of these bigger corporate construction companies, but we have an advantage. The Morrisons have known our family for ages," Leo told Hank.

"But with the town board involved, the local officials and the workers unions, you know as damn well as I do that the board has to follow the rules and get bids from at least three companies," Hank replied.

"You don't sound too hopeful, Hank," Leo said.

"It's not that, it's just I don't want to lose this opportunity," Hank admitted.

"Well I don't want you becoming obsessed with this. Our company has been doing fantastic. I know you want to expand and get out even further, but there are things to consider," Leo replied being honest with Hank about how he felt. He waited for the negative response, the controlling older brother reaction to him giving advice and direction for Hank and for their company. Instead, he heard silence then a long exhale over the phone.

Why was it easier to get things off his chest over the phone than face-to-face with his brother Hank sometimes? It wasn't like Hank intimidated him. Hell, they were brothers. They loved one another, Will included, who was thirty minutes late to work, as usual.

"Listen, the three of us have talked about this. We want to submit a proposal. We're going to submit a proposal and see what happens. If we don't get the job then so be it, but for the next several weeks, we need to get down every detail and think of everything we can to foresee expenses and potential problems so we can correspond with the director. Now, call Will and find out where the hell he is. Then get Adel in here and see if Marcy can cover the front desk for her. We're going to need her assistance through this process," Hank told him.

"Done. I'll be in your office in a few minutes."

Leo ended the call and leaned back in his chair. He could see Adel from here. Her long brown hair was pulled back into some fancy style that ended with a braid over her right shoulder then over her breast. God, she had an amazing body, but she didn't flaunt it. She dressed professionally, conservatively, and there was this aura of maturity, experience, classiness about her that truly made her stand out. Will noticed it. Hell, Hank did, too, but he was fighting his attraction. When would Hank wake up and admit that he wanted to learn more about Adel and make her their woman?

He exhaled as he picked up the phone and called Marcy from inventory. She would have to get coverage for her position while she covered Adel's. It wasn't going to be easy to replace Adel even temporarily. The clients loved her. The suppliers loved her, and anyone who talked to her over the phone felt respected and like they were being cared for as customers. He made the call, exchanged a few pleasantries with Marcy, and ended the conversation just as she started asking about her friend Candice and whether or not he was going to ask her out. Not happening.

He stared out the door that was ajar enough for him to see Adel. She looked beautiful as always, and serious, but there was sadness in her eyes this morning. He felt it in his chest. That uneasy feeling, almost like he felt her sadness and hurt. That was just so extreme. He hadn't even dated her. He'd never kissed her. Hell, he hadn't fucked her although she filled his dreams every night for the past twelve months minimum. Why did he feel such a strong connection to her? What was it about the young woman who showed up in Chance over a year ago that affected him so? Was it those big brown doe eyes, those thick, sexy eyelashes, or maybe just her smile? He wasn't sure, but Will felt it, too, and that had never happened before.

Not like this. Not so powerful. It would be perfect if Hank felt it, too.

He heard the buzzer go off on his desk just as Marcy showed up to replace Adel for the time being. He picked up the phone and answered.

"Yes," he said as he watched the two women exchange pleasantries. Marcy was a redhead, all dolled up, wearing more revealing clothing and less classy than Adel.

"I just pulled into the parking lot. Give me five," Will said, sounding out of breath.

Of course he was late. He'd left Spencer's last night with a redhead on his side and his hand on her ass. Will had a different way of dealing with his attraction to Adel. He tried screwing her out of his head, but pretty damn soon he'd realize it didn't work. Hell, Leo realized that months ago. He hadn't had sex in quite some time. No one got him aroused like Adel and he couldn't even touch her.

Annoyed, he stood up, exhaled, and felt the sick feeling in his gut. Leo consciously made a promise to himself to not sleep with any other women. He would wait for Adel to be ready. Will was on board but dealing with his own ways of ignoring the attraction and trying to find an outlet. Hank? Well, Hank needed to realize there was no fighting the attraction they had with Adel. Hank never dated, rarely screwed around, and was a workaholic. Adel made his eyes light up. She affected him and it would take something major to get him to admit to that attraction and act on it. Leo had to be patient a little longer.

* * * *

Adel showed Marcy some of the paperwork that needed to be filed and calls that were most important to take care of. She felt uneasy about leaving her workstation for many reasons. She didn't like other people doing her job. She also was a bit intimidated by Hank, Leo, and Will. She wished their fathers Harold and William would be present. They made her feel at ease. Probably because it was Harold that talked Hank into giving her this job. He'd known her uncle, Lenny McKinley, for years. They went to college together at Ole Miss. Harold knew what her family did and he knew about her father and dealings with Ross Bentley and his family. Harold didn't care for either man and never had. He especially seemed disgusted with what Bentley had done to her and what her own father had. Her Uncle Lenny asked Harold to keep watch over her and he did. Of course she begged for him not to tell anyone about her past. Harold did. He promised her and she trusted him. It was his sons that she didn't trust or want to get too friendly with. In a lot of ways, Hank reminded her of Bentley and her father. Business came first out of everything, including family.

"Adel, are you ready?" Leo asked, interrupting her thoughts. She had already gathered her laptop and iPad plus her notes and a bottle of water.

"Yes, Mr. Ferguson," she replied and held his gaze. His deep brown eyes seemed to darken at her response to him and then he motioned for her to walk in front of him as he ushered her through the hall to the meeting room. She wondered if he were checking out her ass. She could practically feel his eyes burning her skin and she felt flush. How could she react to him in this way? It wasn't normal. It was like she lusted for the man, for his brothers, yet knew they could be just like Bentley. Besides, her heart couldn't take any more pain and betrayal. Trusting anyone other than herself right now would be too risky.

She locked gazes with Hank, who was already sitting and laying out papers and blueprints.

He glanced at her. His eyes roamed over her breasts and she pressed her palm down the front to ensure nothing was showing. The blouse was a little big. Her nerves and melancholy over the last week were weighing their toll on her figure. Mom called twice and Bentley called three times, including once drunk and with some bimbo giggling in the background telling him to hang up the phone and fuck her already.

She swallowed the bile in her throat, seemingly giving Hank a dirty look before she placed her things down on the table and sat.

"Are you okay, Adel?" Hank asked.

Hank? The silent, brooding, angry boss of a man asked her if she were okay?

"Of course I am. Is Will coming?" she asked.

"Will is here," Will said, entering the office with a laptop and looking rushed but handsome as usual. His brown hair was slicked back, and appeared to be wet as if he just took a shower. The thought made her heart race a little faster.

When he came closer she could smell the soap he used. A cologne-type that had an appealing scent that made her inhale a little deeper. He was sporting a polo shirt today, in black, along with a pair of dress pants. He was into designer clothes and liked to look his best. So did Leo and Hank.

She swallowed hard and opened up her laptop as they exchanged pleasantries.

"You can't be late like this, Will. We've got a lot of work to do to get ready for this proposal. Staying out late on a weeknight can't become a habit," Hank reprimanded.

"Okay, Dad. Sorry I'm late," Will replied sarcastically as he deepened his voice and brought his shoulders to practically to his ears as he shrugged and gave a sorrowful expression.

Leo smirked but caressed the folder in front of him as he stared at her.

She felt her cheeks warm. Those damn dark brown eyes of Leo's and those expressions of authority did a number on her.

"Grow up, Will. Let's get started," Hank said with command and a superiority that was all Hank. The man had the ability to make people stand at attention and keep their eyes focused on him.

Or maybe it was just her? Apparently certain parts of her body had a thing for a man of power. What she didn't like was to be used, abused, and treated like a ready available doormat.

"Let's start with the particulars of the location for the new home development and the surrounding town. It's about thirty minutes south from here. I believe the approximate number of homes to be built is one hundred and fifty homes. Price ranges ranging from low two hundred thousands to over a million. Do you have the details on that, Leo?" Hank looked toward his brother.

Leo opened the file and ran down the list of particulars and the believed time frame to have each phase accomplished.

Adel typed the notes into her computer.

"How many phases are you anticipating and to what amount of homes per phase?" she asked.

"I think working a four-phase schedule would be great, and we could state date of completion earlier," Hank said to them.

"I don't know if that's really feasible and giving enough room for any complications such as delivery mistakes, weather, unforeseen hold-ups. I say five phases," Will added as he started talking about the suppliers they would use, the projects they were currently working on, and the increase in cost of materials.

The three men went back and forth and Adel wondered if she should suggest a more acceptable and rational direction. She'd worked for her father's company from age thirteen and through college where she got her MBA. She knew a lot about construction. In fact she knew the ins and outs and ways to really cut back on costs and to negotiate terms of material prices and so forth, but her job here, the one Harold had gotten her, was personal assistant to these three men, his sons.

One of the things she noticed about the three men was that they liked to handle their sides of the business and not take much constructive criticism. That was fine. They were a privately owned business taking in revenue of over three million a year. If they got this job, that income would double and so would their responsibilities and way of thinking.

She cleared her throat.

"Excuse me. May I make a suggestion?" Adel asked and all three men stopped and stared at her.

Hank looked pissed and also condescending, like he was thinking, "What could she know about this?" Leo gave her his full attention but his jaw was firm as if his brothers' argument was still annoying him, and Will leaned back without a care in the world and an attitude as he crossed his arms in front of his chest and gave the evil eyes to Hank.

"Go ahead, Adel," Leo told her.

She swallowed hard.

"Well, from my initial understanding of this project there will be approximately one hundred and fifty homes being built. Of those homes, only twenty-five of them are mansions, homes over five thousand square feet and in the millions. I think the best thing to do would be to have six phases of development. Take the extra time to split the construction crew to build half of the million-dollar homes after the first phase of the regular homes are built. You want to snag the attention of both types of buyers. Ones in the market for more affordable homes and ones interested in the elite homes. Will could probably come up with an idea to promote both aspects with our advertising department."

"But we would still be on a deadline that would be tough to meet if we spit crews," Hank told her firmly.

"Sir, if you plan on getting this job, you are going to need to double the amount of workers you have now on the payroll. It would be worth it to increase that so that you won't have to increase the time of completion. The Morrisons want all the homes sold before they are even built, so there won't be too much concern over not meeting the deadline. Give yourself leg room and then if all goes according to plan you can tell Morrison you're ahead of schedule and will have it complete before the deadline."

"I like her thinking," Will stated and then he started talking about the way to attack construction. Leo added his comments and she took notes.

She listened to the three brothers go over everything, disagree, resolve the disagreement, and tease one another. As usual, Hank was the more serious one and barely cracked a smile when Leo insulted Will or vice versa.

They were so different, yet a lot alike. She took in Hank's firm expression, his large hands as he held the pen in one and reprimanded his brothers while he jotted things down. He was such a disciplinary man, where Will was a comedian and Leo was an all-around friendly, fun guy.

She felt her cell phone vibrate but ignored it. A few minutes later, as she chuckled at something Will called Leo, she felt her phone vibrate again.

"Do you need to answer that?" Hank asked her, sounding annoyed. She tightened up. Hank had that effect on her.

He raised one of his eyebrows up at her.

"Well, see who it is and if need be take a minute. My brothers are acting like morons and could use the moment to gather their stupidity."

"Hey, Hank, meetings don't have to be constant business and no fun. After all, this is going to be a project with months of these meetings before we even break ground," Will told him as she glanced down at her cell phone.

"We have to get the job first, Will," Hank replied as Adel looked at the caller ID on her cell. She felt that instant sick feeling in her gut. Her face felt as if it went on fire. She was suddenly hot and that meant looking overheated.

*Bentley, you jerk. What in God's name do you want with me? God, could he seriously think I would take him back? After what he did?*

She felt the tears reach her eyes as she quickly turned her cell phone off. That was when she noticed how quiet it got. Slowly she looked up and all three men were staring at her.

"Are you okay?" Will asked her.

She looked away and reached for the laptop to move it closer.

"Yes, of course. So where were we?"

"Is something wrong? Do you need to respond to that message?" Leo asked her, his expression firm, making him appear almost as intimidating as Hank.

She shook her head and placed her fingers on the keyboard, hoping they got the message to continue. When she locked gazes with Hank, figuring it would be easier to make him see she wasn't hiding anything, she was shocked to see the concern in his expression.

"We went over a lot today. We need to go over the time frame, make up the charts on the phases and anything else preliminary before we move onto the blueprints, land structure, and designs. Let's meet back in an hour or so after lunch."

She glanced at her computer screen. It was almost fifteen minutes past one. Had they really been in this meeting that long? She was surprised, but she was relieved to get a breather.

Leo and Will stood up, and she closed the laptop and then reached for her phone and bag.

They didn't say anything to her. She thought maybe one of them might ask about the call or if she were okay, but she must have read into the expressions of concern on their faces. They were probably just annoyed that her phone buzzing interrupted the meeting. So why did that realization make her feel like crap?

She was making herself nuts. One minute she compared these men to Bentley, and pushed any attraction to them away, and the next she was looking for their attention, their care, that apparently she must be creating in her mind. These men didn't care about anything involving her but her professional position in their company. She was alone. Get used to it.

She headed out of the room and felt the phone buzzing again. She glanced at it, wanting to throw it across the room or at minimal, throw it into the small garbage by her desk.

She growled in annoyance as she read the text.

*We need to talk. I'll keep texting. Come on now, Adel. Now.*

Damn it pissed her off so much that he was still making demands on her. She could practically hear his voice, and that demanding ordering tone of his. *Now, Adel. Now!* Screw him.

"Hey, are you okay?" Marcy asked as Alicia reached down to grab her purse that was under the desk

"Fine," she replied.

"That meeting with the three of them was that intense?" Marcy pushed as she eyed over Will when he walked past the desk and to his office. She licked her lips and Adel wanted to smack her.

"No, the meeting with them was fine. Why?"

"Well the three of them have quite the reputations." She moved closer and whispered, "I heard they've had sex in that meeting room with different women."

Adel was shocked and then she was mortified as she covered her hand over her chest.

"Not me," she said on the defensive.

"Of course not you. You're so not their type."

She felt offended now, too. These were too many emotions to feel right now. She should walk away, but she couldn't.

"Why not? What are their type?" she asked.

Marcy smirked.

"Not women with class and brains like you. You're sweet, too. The three of them have reputations as tigers in the bedroom."

"And you know all this how?"

Marcy looked down and then shyly looked back up. "I know people."

"What people do you know? I've lived in Chance longer than you and it's only been like fourteen months for me."

"It's true I tell ya. And, I wouldn't mind it at all. In fact, if one of them asks me for some assistance in their office, I'm making a move. They're loaded, too," she said as she adjusted her cleavage in her blouse.

Adel had enough as she shook her head and laughed even though she wanted to smack Marcy silly.

The protective, jealous feeling was instant. It shocked her as she grabbed her bag. She had to remind herself about men like Hank, Leo, and Will. Well, maybe not so much Leo. He seemed more sincere in his ways. He always asked her how she was feeling and what she did over the weekend. Sometimes she wanted to make shit up.

She headed out of the office and nearly missed the sight of Levi Holmes coming her way. That damn jerk always seemed to be waiting for her, or showed up whenever she was on her way off to lunch or leaving. He gave her the creeps, the way he watched her and showed up all the time, but he never hit on her, or asked her out. He just seemed to want to know where she was going, whom she was with, and what she was up to. She avoided eye contact with him as she saw Steve, one of the guys who worked the construction department.

"Hi, Steve, how are you?" she asked. He smiled wide and let his eyes roam over her body. He was cute, but he drank a lot and from what she heard through the office grapevine, he screwed around a lot, too. He was that no-commitments type of guy, but still very nice to talk to.

"Sweet, sweet, Adel. The question is, how are you?" he teased, noticing Levi and how much the guy unnerved her. Steve placed his arm over her shoulder and whispered into her ear.

"You should really let me kiss you, Adel. That would surely send your stalker running."

She chuckled and went to push on his side for him to release her but he held tight.

"Oh come on, Adel, we'd be good together. Your gorgeous doe eyes and shy, innocent qualities can find protection and security with biceps like mine wrapped around you all the time. We'd be real good together," he whispered, his lips touching her ear.

She laughed, knowing he was such a gigolo, but as she reprimanded him and chuckled, she saw Hank standing there, watching her, and looking like he wanted to kill her.

"You are such a flirt. Do those lines really work with the ladies?" she asked, pushing away from him. She noticed Levi watching and then walking away. At least Steve's acting got Levi to take a walk.

Steve looked over his shoulder, noticing Levi disappeared. He grabbed Adel's hand and brought it to his lips.

"See, my sweet Adel, I told you that would work. Now make this moment perfect and say you'll meet my brothers and I for a few drinks tonight at Spencer's."

She felt her cheeks warm and she definitely was blushing. Steve and his three brothers? No freaking way. Those men were wild.

"Not interested, Steve, but thank you for the help."

He winked at her.

"You're breaking my heart, Adel. My brothers will be disappointed."

She chuckled.

"Something tells me you and your brothers will be just fine. See you later and be safe." She pointed at him.

"Yes, ma'am," he said and she smiled. As she turned around to walk away, Hank was standing there.

"Did you need something before I run out for lunch?" she asked Hank.

Hank looked her body over then stared into her eyes. He was so tall and handsome, but damn was that fierce expression of his powerful. She felt guilty or like she was caught doing something illegal.

He glanced toward Steve, who was walking back toward his department.

"You should be careful around Steve. He's fast and a bit wild," he warned her.

"Steve? He's harmless," she replied and then she noticed Hank seemed to be clenching his teeth or maybe he was biting the inside of his mouth as his cheek sunk in. His eyes grew darker somehow and she gulped.

"You're too good for him and his brothers. Watch yourself," he said with such conviction she took a step back and he immediately walked away.

As she headed out of the building, she felt a multitude of things. She was practically shaking. Hank was a superior man. He also never revealed what was going on in his mind although she was able to pick up on little things over the past several months. When he was upset or angry he got quiet and then he got verbal and demanding. She had witnessed his wrath one time when a group of employees screwed up something on a job site and some workers got hurt. It was something avoidable and he fired the men on the spot. He didn't take chances with his employees' lives. He was a good boss. Hell, he was a good man but not her type. He reminded her of Bentley because of his controlling attitude and fierce way he would look at her. He watched her body or stared at her legs when they were crossed as if he owned her. He liked to sip on expensive brandy, and she didn't know what he was like buzzed never mind drunk.

With Bentley she had been turned on by that attitude and possessiveness, but too soon that possessiveness made her feel like an object, like something he owned and could do what he wished with. The love, the compassion, the care was replaced with being manhandled, somewhat abused by his firm grips, not-so-gentle tugs and pushes, and of course Bentley's verbal orders and demands. Throw in some alcohol and the man turned into a monster. How her father didn't seem to care made her wonder if he ever really loved her as his daughter.

She felt the tears reach her eyes and she put on her sunglasses as she walked down the block. She forced herself to not think of Bentley, or to analyze Hank, or fantasize about Leo, wondering what kind of lover he would be, and she didn't think about Will, who was wild and a playboy.

The best thing to do was to avoid an attraction to her bosses. To not get involved with any men from work, and to just put her past behind her and not think of the painful memories any more.

She stopped by the deli in town and grabbed a salad and an ice tea. It was beautiful out today and considering she would be stuck in the meeting room with her bosses for the rest of the afternoon, she should enjoy lunch outside.

As she found a spot near the small park, she set up her things and pulled out her iPad. She saw text messages from Alicia and Marlena and then her phone went off as Mercedes texted her. She read the texts from Mercedes.

*Going to Spencer's tonight for a few drinks with Alicia and Marlena. You have to come, too. I can't be stuck with all their men and feeling like I'm the single tag-a-long friend. Pleaseee.*

Adel chuckled. Mercedes was so funny, and she was right. Adel went out with Alicia and Marlena a few times with their men and she felt out of place. Their men were touching them, kissing them, and being affectionate. That made the one single girl not only feel out of place but also in the spotlight for loser guys to come over thinking she was desperate for a man . She texted back immediately.

*Sure thing. I'll meet you there at 7:00.*

Adel began to eat her lunch and in between she searched online for a new ceiling fan for her bedroom. The damn thing broke it was so old and considering her small cottage didn't have central air , she only had a window AC unit and the bedroom fan to keep her cool at night. She needed one desperately.

"So this is where you disappear for lunch."

She gasped and looked up to see Will standing there and holding a brown bag and an ice tea. His hazel eyes were blocked by some designer sunglasses that hid his eyes completely.

She didn't know what to say but he sure did.

"Can I join you?" he asked, taking a seat and setting up his stuff alongside her.

"Sure. I guess," she replied and then looked back at her iPad and noticed the prices for some of the basic fans. She exhaled.

"What are you looking at fans for?" he asked, and then bit into a large sub sandwich.

She turned to look at him. He removed his sunglasses and his hazel eyes held hers a moment. She could smell his cologne or was it the damn appealing soap he used in the shower this morning? She thought about the way he looked as he ran into the meeting room. His hair was practically still dripping. He must have been out late last night. Or maybe up all night. Was he alone in bed, or had some lucky woman gotten whisked off her feet by the very handsome and charming Will Ferguson?

She swallowed hard. He wasn't her type either. A playboy who slept with a lot of women just because he could.

"Mine broke. I need a replacement one," she told him then scrolled down to a cheaper one.

"Do you really need one? Doesn't your cottage have AC?" he asked.

She shook her head. "Just a small unit in the window. It's supposed to get hotter next week and I'll be miserable if I don't get a new one installed right away."

"If you don't mind one in brown or white, I think we have some overstock in storage from the last construction site."

"How much?"

He smiled.

"You don't have to pay for it."

"No, I couldn't do that. They were all paid for originally. What is the price? I'm on a limited budget."

"Why is that? We pay you really well," he asked. God he was so forward. He hadn't a clue about struggling to make ends meet. He had money most of his life. She was on her own now and left home with five thousand dollars to her name. She couldn't tell him how she needed a new dryer and was hang-drying her clothing outside. She couldn't tell him her oven was leaking gas and she had to disconnect it because she didn't want to blow up the small cottage she now owned. It was tough but she needed to be independent.

She felt the hand on her knee and Will gave it a squeeze. Immediately her breasts felt full, her nipples hardened, and her pussy was on alert. All from a simple touch.

She instinctively pushed his hand off her knee and scooted slightly to the right.

He looked insulted, maybe hurt, and she turned away.

"Adel, let me help you out with the fan. If you want to give the company fifty bucks to feel better about it then do it. I can get over to your place to install it this weekend," he told her then took another bite of his lunch.

She was shocked that he offered and realizing how she reacted to his touch, there was no way she could let him in her home never mind her bedroom to fix the fan.

"That's okay. Steve said he could help me out with any installations I need."

He squinted his eyes at her and seemed pissed off. "Steve is not going to your place to *help* you with anything." He emphasized the word help like there was so much more meaning to it. Then it hit her. He knew Steve flirted with her. Maybe Will thought Steve would make a move at her place. Hell, Steve would make a move on her at her place and especially in the bedroom.

She worried her lower lip.

"Maybe you're right. Steve is a flirt and he could take me asking for his help the wrong way, but you wouldn't do that," she challenged him and tried to read his facial expression.

"Of course not. You're our personal assistant. My brothers and I have told you numerous times that if you need any help with anything, just ask."

"Of course, but if you're sure you're not too busy. I mean I know how you enjoy a lot of parties and social events on the weekend."

He appeared insulted at her comment.

"Not this weekend. Helping you comes first," he said then took another bite of his sandwich. She closed her iPad and then finished her lunch.

"So, any plans for tonight?" he asked.

"Just meeting my friends at Spencer's for a few drinks."

He smiled.

"Well, I could get that fan for you and come over to your cottage tomorrow if you want? It won't take long to install."

"Tomorrow? That soon?" she asked, surprised that he could get it done that quickly.

"Sure. How about eleven? Will that give you enough recovery time from drinking tonight?" he asked with a smirk.

"I don't tend to drink a lot. In fact, I don't like being around people who drink a lot either. It makes me uncomfortable," she told him.

"Well, I don't blame you. People sometimes act differently when they're drunk."

"Yeah, some people act like idiots and can be hurtful."

"Sounds like you've had some experiences with that?"

She looked at him and those sexy hazel eyes, the way he sat there appearing so big, so accomplished and capable. She let the words leave her lips without thinking.

"I've seen people do some terrible things when they're drunk. Even the nicest guys could turn into monsters."

As his eyes widened and then scrunched together she realized what she said. She was thinking about Bentley and how he hit her, grabbed her forcefully, and made demands on her in a drunken state.

"Hey, are you okay?" he asked her as he placed his arm over the back of her chair. She felt his thumb caress against her bare skin on her arm and she cleared her throat.

"I'm great, but I think lunch is over. I'd hate to get your brother angry by showing up late." She started gathering her things and he seemed hesitant to leave. Was he enjoying their conversation?

As they stood up and gathered their garbage, Will touched her hand.

"Hey, not all guys are assholes. Sometimes alcohol just reveals who they really are."

"You don't have to tell me," she said and chuckled as they began walking back to the office together. As they got to the sidewalk toward the front door her phone rang.

She answered it without looking at the caller ID.

"Hey, baby. I've missed your voice."

She heard Bentley's words and his voice and she stopped short. Tears hit her eyes and Will stopped short.

"Adel, are you there?" he asked.

"Excuse me. I need to take this call," she told Will.

He nodded and she turned around and headed to the side a bit.

"Why are you calling me? I told you not to," she stated firmly.

"Baby, don't be like that. I'm worried about you, and so are your parents."

"Yeah well, I'm fine and I certainly don't need you checking up on me."

"But I care about you. I worry about you. Are you working?"

"That's none of your business. I asked you to leave me alone. Why can't you just do that?"

"Because I still love you, baby. I want to talk to you and make things up to you."

"Bye." She clicked the phone off and exhaled. The tears hit her eyes and she growled low.

That son of a bitch. *Why can't he just leave me alone? What does he want from me?*

"Adel?" She felt the hand on her shoulder and instinctively, she abruptly turned around and was shocked to lock gazes with Will. He looked concerned and she closed her eyes and kept her hands at her side.

She felt his hands caress her arms and held her there. Her eyes popped open.

"Do you want to talk about it?"

She shook her head.

"Do you need my help?"

"No, Will. I'm sorry. It's personal. I'll be fine. I can take care of it."

"Are you sure?" he asked, reaching for her chin and tilting her face up toward him so she could lock gazes with him.

"Yes, Will, I have to be."

She turned away from him and headed inside.

\* \* \* \*

Will watched Adel walk away and he was concerned to say the least. Whomever called her was obviously bothering her and not listening to her request to leave her alone. Was it an ex-boyfriend? Was the guy abusive? Maybe someone who drank a lot and hurt her? His mind was assuming so many things after their nice conversation during lunch and what she shared. Hell, if her ex—well, if there was an ex—who drank a lot and was abusive to her then he would give up drinking if it made her uncomfortable. He wanted to know who the guy was. He wanted to help her and to take the look of fear, of anger and sadness from her eyes. He had to talk to his brothers.

They had all witnessed her taking calls from her mom and how sad she got. They knew nothing about her family, her past, or even where she worked before. Their father Harold knew her and recommended giving her the job. They accepted their father's good judgment and they hadn't been disappointed since. In fact, they spent more time around her than they needed to. Having her help with this new business venture was a plus. He needed to talk to Leo. If some guy was harassing her, together they would take care of him and protect Adel. She was going to be theirs eventually. They just needed to gain her trust and prove to her that they weren't going to hurt her.

He felt sick. What if Adel had been abused? What if the guy still wanted her? He had to find out. He exhaled and entered the building searching for Leo and Hank, but it was time to meet again in the meeting room and Adel was already there looking professional and ready. Her smile seemed sincere, but he knew she was hiding her emotions. Something was going on and he and his brothers would get to the bottom of it.

# Chapter 2

Adel looked around Spencer's as she sipped on a glass of white wine. She wasn't in the mood for drinking, for socializing for that matter. Bentley called her again and it was making her crazy. Why did he want to know where she was working and if she was handling things okay? She just wanted to be left alone and to have the past behind her, but she was uptight, on edge, and it didn't help that Steve was here and so were his brothers. All four of them were watching her, and then she saw Will and Leo. She swallowed hard. They stood out in a crowd with their designer dress pants and solid polo shirts. Add in their attitudes, the way they walked around like they owned the place, and oh yeah, they grabbed every woman's attention in the place.

"Hey, beautiful, will your friends let you leave them long enough for me to buy you a drink?" Steve asked, interrupting her zoned out time. She felt embarrassed and hoped no one noticed her staring at two of her bosses.

Mercedes raised one of her eyebrows up at him. "Are you kidding me? And leave me to fend on my own with these lovebirds surrounding us?"

Adel laughed and so did Steve. He reached both hands out to the two of them.

"Come on both of you. We'll buy you a drink."

Mercedes took Steve's hand and so did Adel and then they walked with them toward his brothers and some group of guys. Adel noticed Deputy Taylor Dawn, out of uniform of course, and two of his brothers, Kurt and Warner. Their eyes immediately roamed over Mercedes and she looked away from them.

Adel had the feeling that the Dawn brothers were interested in Mercedes. Warner and Kurt were pretty mysterious men who had military pasts. She could remember hearing some gossip about them being spies and very resourceful. Mercedes worked in the sheriff's department so she probably heard things, too. Mercedes had a hard childhood and young adult life, so Adel could understand her fears. Hers were similar. If she couldn't trust her own father and mother, how could she ever trust any man?

Adel felt the hand on her lower back and then Steve whisper next to her ear.

"What are you drinking?"

"Oh, I'm good actually. I've been sipping this all night."

"Maybe you need something different?" he asked.

"Yeah, like one of those girly drinks your friend Marlena is sipping," Caleb, Steve's brother, suggested as he nodded toward Marlena where they'd just left. Then his eyes roamed over her body again. She felt self-conscious and she also realized that she wasn't attracted to any of these men.

"I'm good for now, but thank you," she replied. She glanced to the right, back to where she had seen Leo and Will but they were no longer there. She felt disappointed and then she felt like an idiot. Why was she paying attention to them and worried about where they were? Leo and Will were all wrong for her and they were out of her league. She took a sip of wine and listened to Mercedes correct the story that Taylor was explaining of a recent burglary attempt not far from where she lived. They had gotten some new evidence and even a lead in the case.

Adel couldn't help but to smile. As much as Mercedes tried to hide her attraction to Taylor, Kurt, and Warner, they tried even harder making it obvious that all four of them were interested.

"Good evening, everyone." She heard the voice and felt the hands on her shoulders at the same time. She nearly spilled her drink.

Will approached along with Leo as Will pressed up against her back.

The men greeted him and Leo as Leo took position right next to her and winked, then smiled before he took a sip of his beer.

Will's hands massaged her shoulders and then she felt his lips next to her ear.

"I got that fan we talked about. I'll meet you at your place at eleven?" he asked but it seemed Steve had heard him. Steve squinted his eyes and Adel could hardly breathe having Will this close to her and smelling so good. His hands felt amazing on her shoulders and she wished she were wearing something that covered them completely instead of the tank style blouse.

She looked at him and nodded her head.

"If you're sure it's no problem. I mean if you have plans or something it's no big deal. I could get someone to help me install it."

"The fan? Heck, Will, if you've got some hot date or want to take your boat out for the day, I'd be happy to help Adel install a new fan in her bedroom. It's the bedroom right?" Steve asked and held her gaze. She could tell he was flirting as usual, but Will didn't find it amusing and nor did Leo as Will squeezed her shoulders again and then released them and stood on her other side.

"No. We've got this covered. Adel comes before everything else," he said and she looked at Will like he was crazy, but Will had that firm Ferguson expression on his face that made her pull her bottom lip between her teeth and wonder why he was being so intense. His tone was different than when they were in the office.

She watched expressions exchange between all of the men. Then suddenly Steve looked affected and then looked at Will and Leo then back to Will.

"Since when," Steve asked in regards to her coming before everything.

"For quite some time," Leo replied.

"Do we need to discuss this in private?" Will asked, placing his hand at her lower back.

Adel locked gazes with Mercedes, who looked shocked. What was Adel missing here? It was like some silent conversation was going on about her and she was the one out of the loop.

"Might be," Steve replied, crossing his arms in front of his chest.

"Really? Because I'm thinking there isn't anything to discuss at all," Leo said with attitude.

"What's going on here? Did I miss something in this conversation?" she asked.

The men seemed to all rein in their anger and their expressions softened.

"Not at all, Adel. So what do you say? Girlie drink?" Steve asked her.

"No, I'm good, really, but thank you, and thank you for offering to help with the fan, but considering Will got it I guess it makes sense for him to install it."

"Yeah, I guess it does," Steve said and then looked Will over, giving him the evil eye.

She looked at Mercedes and shrugged her shoulders. Mercedes smiled.

"What time will you be done installing the fan, Will? Adel and I have plans to hit the lake for some sun and relaxing time," Mercedes asked him.

"No more than an hour," he replied. Then looked Adel over. "Maybe a little longer."

Adel felt her cheeks warm. It was instant but that was the effect Will had on her.

"That sounds like fun. Are you ladies headed to the lake near Marlena's place?" Warner asked.

"Yes, you know it?" Adel asked.

"Of course we do. We've gone to another one a mile down the road from where your cottage is, Adel," Steve told her.

"If you guys want to come along you can. I think we're trying to organize the food and some hibachis to BBQ down there and maybe set up a campfire in the evening. It should be fun," Mercedes added.

"We can bring along some food and an extra grill," Taylor chimed in and Mercedes looked at him and tightened her lips.

"Oh this will be a lot of fun with so many of us. Maybe you want to come along, too, Will, Leo?" Adel asked because she felt funny not asking them as everyone else around them started inviting themselves along.

"We'll see. Maybe," Leo said.

"I'll be there. I'll bring some stuff with me to your place and my brothers can meet us there if they decide to go, too," Will said to her and she smiled.

She looked around at the others and felt a bit of tension still and wasn't certain why. One look at Mercedes and she seemed to know as a small smile formed on her lips and she winked at Adel. What did Mercedes know that she didn't know?

\* \* \* \*

At 10:50 in the morning, Adel heard the pickup truck pull up in front of her cottage. She could see the truck reversing backward up the small driveway and the big box in the back of the truck. The picture of the ceiling fan looked big and she wondered if it would fit.

She opened the screen door and greeted Will as he got out of the truck. He smiled wide. She was wearing a sun dress with her bathing suit underneath it.

"Hi, Will."

"Good morning, Adel. You look pretty as always," he said to her.

She smiled and said thank you as she met him at the back of his truck. Will of course looked amazing. He wore a pair of jeans and a tight navy blue T-shirt that showed off his pectoral muscles. He towered over her as she stood in flip flops and asked if he needed help as he let the tail gate down.

"Not at all. You just stay looking beautiful while I get this thing inside."

She noticed the picture on the box and she gasped. This fan was an expensive fan. More like five hundred dollars than fifty dollars and that was at wholesale prices for large numbers of inventory.

"Will, I can't take this. That's got a copper finish and real wood and those light covers are made of hand-blown glass. The covers alone are more than fifty dollars."

"Adel, don't worry about it. The fans are just sitting there collecting dust and eventually will be tossed out or used elsewhere. This is a great fan and will help keep you comfortable on those hot, summer nights," he said and lifted the box.

She held the door open as he brought the box into the small living room. She was embarrassed about him seeing her small place. His place was big. He and his brothers had a huge house with lots of property and only a block from the beach.

"I don't think the box is going to fit down this hallway. This is cute, Adel," he told her as he looked at her. He appeared so big, too big in her small living room.

"It's perfect for me, considering I live alone. I don't need much," she said, feeling embarrassed as she lowered her head. She felt his fingers under her chin and she immediately looked up toward him.

"Hey, it's perfect for one person. So where's your bedroom?" he asked and she gulped.

Since leaving Spencer's last night with Mercedes she was feeling a bit nervous. Mercedes believed that Will and Leo were setting the groundwork for claiming Adel as their woman, and Steve and his brothers were pissed about it because they liked her, too. The thought had her up most of the night. Where Steve and his brothers showed their interest in her, or at least Steve did at work by flirting, Will,

Hank, and Leo did not. They complimented her here and there and seemed to be concerned whenever she wasn't smiling, and even now, Will offered to help with the fan, but he did agree that he wasn't flirting with her. He didn't want Steve installing the fan because Steve was a flirt. That was the only reason why Will volunteered.

"I just need to grab my tools. Also, do you know where the main circuit breaker box is? I'll need to turn off the line going to this fan."

"Sure. I'll show you. It's in the small room in the back."

She calmed herself down and rationalized the situation as Will grabbed his tools. Fifteen minutes later he was struggling to get the old fan down and noticed some faulty wiring.

"This isn't good, Adel. The wiring is all bad. I'll have to replace this but I don't know if I can do that without breaking into the sheetrock to get to the main hookups. It looks like the previous owner must have swapped out the new fan with an old one."

"Figures. This place was on the market for quite some time but it fit my budget when I first got here. I can always get someone to come back and fix the sheetrock. I probably could do it myself."

"You? Not happening. I'll do it or even Leo. He's great at spackling and taping, too. He'll make it look like nothing ever happened."

She heard her phone ringing.

"Go answer that. I'll be a bit trying to get this sucker down."

She walked out of the room and answered the phone.

"When I tell you to call me you'd better do it. Now enough is enough, Adel. We need to talk."

"No, we don't. I've got nothing to say to you. What don't you understand about that?" she asked, raising her voice.

"You're awfully mouthy. You don't want to piss me off, Adel."

"Or what? You'll hit me? I'm not afraid of you. Just leave me alone and stop calling me."

"Never, Adel. I'll make your life a living hell. I want you back."

"Never happening. Leave me alone." She disconnected the call and threw her phone onto the couch. She covered her face with her hands.

"Adel." She heard Will's voice and gasped, instantly feeling embarrassed. He must have heard her phone call. Oh God what he must be thinking.

She turned toward him and wiped her eyes before the tears fell and forced a smile.

"Were you able to get it? Do you need help?" she asked and went to walk by him but Will grabbed her arm to stop her. He stared down into her eyes, his expression of concern and sympathy.

"Who was that? Is someone bothering you? A man?"

"Please don't ask me any questions. I'm fine. I've got this."

She attempted to pull free slightly, but he held firm.

"Talk to me. I can help you if you confide in me."

She shook her head.

"I can't."

"You can't, or you won't?" he pushed.

"I can't."

"Why not?"

"Because you're a man. Because you're not even a friend. You're my boss."

He shook his head and pulled her close.

"I don't just want to be your boss or your friend. I want more than that."

Her eyes widened and she went to pull back but he drew her in closer.

"What are you talking about? Stop fooling around, Will." She chuckled softly but it was lame. His comment affected her and had her wondering why he said that.

"Adel, look at me. You can't be so oblivious to the way I feel about you. Come on, even Leo was making certain that Steve wouldn't get a chance to be alone with you."

He reached out and cupped her cheek, then ran his thumb along her chin.

"I made certain it would be me here today changing this fan and being the only man in your bedroom."

"But you're my boss. Why would you and Leo do that? What kind of game are you playing, Will? I don't play games."

He wrapped his arm around her waist and cupped her hair and neck with his other hand and held her gaze. His eyes roamed over her lips and the cleavage of the tank top she wore. "You sure aren't. You're special. You're everything my brothers and I need in our lives and have searched for."

"Don't say such things. Quit it, Will." She tried to push him away but his expression firmed as his eyebrows burrowed.

"You don't think I'm serious? You haven't noticed the way Leo looks at you or how jealous Hank gets when Steve or any other male employee talks to you?"

"Your brothers aren't interested in me, and certainly not Hank. He hardly even speaks to me."

He chuckled low. "Hank is so into you he doesn't even want to admit it out loud. He'll come around. He has trust issues." He leaned down as if he might kiss her.

"Don't, Will. This will make matters worse for me right now."

"Worse for you how? Is someone bothering you? Threatening you? An ex? Who is he?"

"Please, Will, don't ask me questions. I'm not going to tell you anything. It's none of your business. You're my boss."

"But I want to be more than that."

"Why are you doing this? Why me? You can have your choice of any woman you want and so can your brothers. Hell, Will, I've cancelled dates for you. I've made excuses over the phone for you and your brothers so you could avoid seeing a woman you slept with ever again. How can you expect me to take you serious?"

"That was months ago, besides, we all have different ways of trying to get you out of our heads. Maybe mine was stupid, and I realize that now because no woman, no other person compares to you. What will it take to prove that we're serious about getting to know you and taking this to the next level?"

She held his gaze. Stared into his hazel eyes and tried to see if he was telling the truth or just being Will, the bachelor, the out-for-a-good-time kind of guy.

He brushed his thumb along her lower lip.

"You're killing me here. I want to taste you, Adel. Let me kiss you and see if you feel what I'm feeling."

He lowered his mouth closer and closer to hers. A few different reasons why not to kiss him entered her mind but only for a moment. Then his lips touched hers.

She felt his firm, masculine lips press against her own and at first she was shocked and scared. As his hand massaged along her waist and she absorbed the scent of his cologne and the feel of his muscles she began kissing him back.

But then her mind traveled over the things that had occurred in her life and the pain that Bentley, and her own father, had caused her and she panicked. How could any man love her when her own father didn't?

She pushed against his chest and he released her lips. She covered her mouth and shook her head.

"Baby, please. Talk to me, Adel. Don't fight this."

She uncovered her mouth.

"I should have stopped you. We shouldn't have kissed. I'm not good for you. You're not good for me."

"You're so wrong, Adel. You're perfect."

She felt the tears reach her eyes as she pushed away from him.

"Adel."

She turned toward him.

"I'm not perfect. I'm not interested in playing your games. That shouldn't have happened."

He stepped closer and she stepped back.

He looked upset, hurt, and she felt badly but she needed to stand her ground. This wasn't good. She was so confused.

"I want to talk to you about this. About that phone call."

"No, Will. Let's forget both ever happened. Now can you do that and fix the fan or do I need to get someone else to?" She held her ground and he looked her over. He ran his fingers under his lip as if contemplating his next move or the right reply.

"Steve is not allowed in this house, never mind in your bedroom." He walked back down the hallway and she felt like crying. Hell, like screaming. What was she going to do? Will kissed her. She kissed him. He was one of her bosses. Oh God, she'd have to find a new job. How the hell would she do that? No one was hiring, and this was right in town. *Damn you, Bentley. Damn you!*

\* \* \* \*

"Okay spill the beans. What the heck happened between you and that sexy man Will?" Mercedes asked as Adel joined her and the others down by the water. Despite the bad way things went down with her and Will, he and Leo showed up and they brought beer, food to cook up, and a grill big enough to cook everything.

"I don't want to talk about it."

"Why not? Is it that bad?" Mercedes asked and Adel nodded her head.

It was hot out and everyone was either in the water or making their way in.

"Well whatever happened it sure didn't change their minds about coming here. I wonder where Hank is. He's the oldest right?"

Adel nodded her head.

"He's the one that doesn't really socialize but works out a lot? Martial arts I think I heard Taylor say."

"Oh, speaking of Deputy Taylor and his brothers, how did things go? Did they ask you out?"

"Oh God no. That is not going to happen."

"Why do you say that?"

"Because I'm too young for them, I work in the Sheriff's office, and everyone would feel awkward. Taylor gives me the evil eyes whenever one of the deputies flirts with me. Then when I'm out, like at Spencer's, and Kurt and Warner are there, they give me dirty looks and then they stare at whomever I'm with, making the guys feel uncomfortable. It's like a silent message to leave me alone."

"Okay, so I don't see the problem."

"They aren't serious about me. Would you consider a ménage relationship, sex with three or even four men, if they were only looking for a good time and to explore an attraction? I know I don't want to walk around Chance with a 'used goods' sign plastered on my forehead. No thank you."

Adel thought about what Mercedes said and she realized she feared the same thing. When she thought about entertaining an attraction to Will, she immediately thought about his brothers, too. It was like they were all connected. How would she face her friends and the employees at the company if Will, Leo, and Hank used her for sex? She would have to quit. She'd have to face Harold, their dad, and he knew the truth about what happened to her. He knew her father chose Bentley over her and that Bentley cheated on her and abused her. Harold would be disappointed and think maybe she was trying to use his sons for their wealth and connections.

"I know what you mean, and you're right. I think we both need to be cautious and not take any chances with any men until we're certain."

Mercedes nodded toward the men as a group of them, including Taylor, Kurt, Warner, Leo, and Will, removed their shirts, showing off their sexy muscular bodies before they made their way into the water.

"Or until we become too aroused and needy to even care," Mercedes said very seriously and Adel agreed and they both looked at one another and started laughing.

* * * *

"So you never got anything out of Adel about the caller?" Leo asked Will.

"No, things turned badly once I kissed her. It was like she freaked out and panicked. She sounded so insecure and untrusting, like we would use her and leave her for scraps."

"What? Why the hell would she respond like that? We haven't given her the impression that we would treat her like crap. This would be a big risk getting personal with our personal assistant," Leo said then chuckled.

"Yeah, I want to get real personal with her and this waiting is killing me, but she's scared, and it's obvious someone hurt her."

Leo scrunched his eyes together as they stood in the water up to their chests. He ran the water along his arms and shoulders.

"You think someone hurt her, like abused her or you mean broke her heart?"

"She's an old-fashioned kind of girl. I think maybe both. If you heard the emotion in her voice as she took that phone call you would know what I mean. She sounded scared and like she was trying to be tough."

"She can trust us though. You told her that we're all interested?"

"She didn't believe me. She even said that Hank never says a word to her or shows interest in that way and nor do you."

"That's because we didn't want to come on too strong, but maybe we should step on the gas a little here?"

"I'm not sure, Leo, but I can tell you this, her kisses are addicting. What I would do right now just to hold her in my arms and kiss her."

They heard the squeal and then looked toward the water's edge to see Mercedes, Adel, Alicia, and Marlena along with a few other women. Steve was filling up water guns and shooting them.

They were all laughing as everyone reached for a water gun and tried to fill it up. It was such a childish game to play but as Will caught sight of Adel running to hide with a water gun in hand he winked at Leo and they both made their way toward the shoreline to grab a water gun.

Of course there were smaller ones left but that didn't matter.

"We'll sneak around and get her on both sides," Leo said and they filled the guns then ran up the beach and over the grass just as Adel came around the tree. To their surprise she had water balloons and threw them right at them one after the next.

Will got hit in the shoulder and Leo got hit in the head. Instead of stopping, Leo charged.

"Oh you're in trouble now, Miss McKinley," Leo told her and Adel screamed and laughed as Leo chased her.

In a flash he lifted her up and threw her over his shoulder.

"Leo! Put me down. Put me down," she said but was laughing.

"Oh no, Adel, you're in for it now," Will said and squirted her with the water gun a few times as Leo brought her to the water.

"Wait, wait. I need to take off my cover-up. I don't have a change of clothes."

"Oh well, we'll think of something later," Leo said and then ran with her over his shoulder into the water, her sundress and all, and dunked her.

She came up laughing and then splashing him. The others were carrying on and still shooting the water guns and even starting a game of volleyball. Will watched as Leo pulled her closer and brought her deeper into the lake and away from the crowd. His brother would make a few steps forward in the progress department. Will was certain of that as he slowly took his time to join them.

\* \* \* \*

Leo's heart was racing inside of his chest. The feel of Adel in his arms was more than he anticipated. Her laughter brightened his mood and those damn big brown doe eyes did a number on him every time.

He held her close and then she pushed back. "I have to get this off. It's making me sink."

She struggled to get the sundress off and when she finally removed it with his help, he saw how well-endowed she was and how tiny and sexy her little purple floral bikini was.

He took the dress from her, squeezed it out, and tossed it to Will, who rolled his eyes, took it, and brought it back toward the shoreline to hang it to dry. That would give Leo some more alone time with Adel.

She was trying to keep herself afloat and he could still touch the bottom so he pulled her closer.

"I've got you. Hold onto my shoulders."

"Leo, we shouldn't."

He pulled her against him and she placed her hands on his shoulders.

"We should. It's fine. Nice and slow, Adel. We're just friends having some fun, getting to know one another out of the workplace."

She rolled her eyes at him, not believing a word he was saying.

"What, you don't believe me?" he challenged, trying to keep his voice steady when he felt it shaking. She was voluptuous yet petite and feminine. She smelled incredible and her body was to die for. He could feel his cock harden and he prayed she didn't feel it or she might panic.

"Did you know that my favorite color is purple?" he teased and let his eyes roam over her cleavage then to her lips and eyes.

"No, I didn't."

He pulled her closer.

"Really? Are you sure?" he asked as the water rocked between them and around them, adding to the vibrations of desire traveling through his body. He wanted to kiss her. He wanted to explore her curves and sink his cock into her sweet pussy right here, right now.

"If I did then I would have worn my red one," she said to him and looked away as if bored by his flirty comments. Will was closing in and within earshot.

"Well that would have been fine, too. Will loves red."

"Red what?" Will asked, joining them.

"Red bikinis. Red lingerie, red thongs, hell, red anything," Leo teased. She looked serious and pressed her hands to his shoulders.

"Whoa, baby, I was only teasing like you teased me."

"Really?"

"What, you can dish it out but can't take it?"

"Teasing I can take. Games, lies, I don't have tolerance for."

"Well either do we, so that's a good thing," he said to her and held her gaze. She stared at him, making him feel like he was under some sort of probe light and could see any indication of lie or ulterior motive. God she was so beautiful. She was making him nuts.

"No games, Adel. I promise. So tell me, do you like the new fan in your bedroom?" he asked.

"It's okay. Not really my taste," she told him and Will was shocked as he widened his eyes and splashed her.

She laughed and Leo felt it in his chest. That sweet rumbling sound of her laughter colliding with the beat of his heart. He was losing his mind.

Will tickled her and she swatted at his hands and then he stopped.

"Okay. I was kidding. I love it. It's too fancy for my little cottage but I love it."

"Well it's perfect for your bedroom and will do its job."

"Which I am glad at, because tonight is going to be a hot one."

"I'm just glad I didn't have to break the sheetrock to get it installed. I was worried. What a mess that would have been."

"I appreciate that, Will. That would have led to me repainting the bedroom. No time for that."

Leo maneuvered her closer and Will bumped into her. They heard more laughter.

"Looks like everyone is having fun. This was a great idea," Leo told her.

"Yeah, we were looking forward to just relaxing in the sun and swimming in the water just enjoying it."

Leo maneuvered her to her back and she gasped.

He held her with his arms under her back and legs.

"Lean back and relax. I won't let you sink." She seemed shy and shocked at the same time.

Will caressed her hair from her shoulders.

"We've got you. Close your eyes and enjoy the sun and the water."

She leaned back and closed her eyes and Leo and Will looked at her body, at the reflection of sunlight glistening over the top of the water and right to Adel. The pretty purple, floral bikini was stylish and sexy. The top dipped low and the bikini bottoms showed off her firm belly and her toned, tan thighs. She was so beautiful. Like a water angel.

She raised her arms up and back, causing her breasts to lift upward. Her fingertips touched the water and then she shot the water back at both of them.

Leo released her as she squealed and then she started swimming away, but Leo grabbed her ankle and pulled her back, causing her to laugh even louder. He pulled her close, turned her away from the inquiring eyes, and kissed her.

The water was deeper where they stood and she wrapped her legs around his waist, making him moan into her mouth as he ran his hands along her ass and her back. The kiss grew wild and then slowed down. He held her bottom lip between his teeth gently before releasing them. The sight of her took his breath away. Light tiny drips of water trickled from her thick, long eyelashes, and along her nose and over her plump, wet lips.

"Just as I imagine in my dreams, you taste even better, Adel."

\* \* \* \*

Adel was trying to catch her breath. Here she was with her legs wrapped around her boss Leo's waist. Her other boss Will was pressed up against her back, caressing her arms and her friends were mere feet away enjoying a game of volleyball, but her body wanted more. She wanted to disappear into the woods and explore their bodies and these emotions she was feeling. It was all too much.

"Oh God, Leo, Will, what are we doing?"

She felt Will's hands on her waist from behind and then his lips touched her shoulder.

"What we've wanted to do for quite some time. Taste you, spend time with you, and be close to you."

She held Leo's gaze. He licked his lower lip as his eyes trailed over her breasts then to her lips. She was on fire. Her pussy throbbed, her nipples hardened to tiny buds. This was overwhelming. No man ever made her feel this way, not even Bentley, and she almost married him.

The thought upset her as she pushed Leo away and moved to the side. Will went to reach for her but she waded in the water and held one hand up. She moved closer toward the shoreline where she could stand.

"Don't push us away. Don't minimize what you felt and what we felt."

Her thoughts were frazzled.

"I'm not. I mean, I don't know what to think and how to process this. I can't right now. I can't do this." She was going to swim toward the others but Leo grabbed her hand to stop her.

"Slow down."

"Does this have something to do with the call from earlier today?" Will asked. She looked at him and felt the tears in her eyes. If she never met Bentley, never had a father who didn't love her, maybe she could give this nontraditional type of relationship a try.

"Will...yes," she said. She was going to try to deny it but she just couldn't lie to them.

Leo pulled her closer and she tried to resist. He was so big and muscular and had this tattoo along his upper arm and shoulder. All three brothers shared such intense dark expressions. He cupped her cheek.

"Is somebody bothering you? Because if so, you need to tell us, or tell Max, someone, so you don't get hurt. Baby, you can trust us."

She shook her head.

"I can't."

"You won't," Will interjected and took her other hand. He brought it to his lips and kissed her knuckles. She stared into hazel eyes and so badly she wanted to trust them, to tell them she was scared and she didn't want to get hurt.

"This guy, the one calling you, he hurt you?" Leo asked her.

She looked away. "God, please, Leo, don't do this to me. This is why I can't get involved with you or Will."

"And Hank, too. We all want you," Will added.

She shook her head.

"Hank isn't interested in me. Forget that. It doesn't matter. I'm sorry, but you just need to accept the fact that now is not a good time for me to engage in some free-for-all. I'm not like that. I'm not the kind of woman you guys get involved with."

"Whoa, slow down and wait one minute. You're exactly what we've ever wanted in a woman to share."

"Please, Leo, give me some credit will ya," she said and pulled back. "I've taken the phone calls, I've heard the gossip."

"What gossip?" Will pushed. He stood there looking at her like she was nuts meanwhile he and his brothers had reputations as playboys. Well except for Hank. He was just known as a mean hard ass who probably was into kinky stuff. She swallowed hard. The thought aroused her and it shouldn't. What were these men doing to her?

"You like us, and you're making excuses," Leo pushed.

"No, I'm not. I won't be some woman who you get to screw whenever you want to and even in the meeting room at work."

"What?" Leo and Will both asked, raising their voices and drawing attention to the three of them.

She felt her cheeks warm as she lowered her eyes and then moved back a little.

She whispered as she glanced around to be sure no one heard her, "The meeting room table? I heard the gossip about you having sex in there with different women, okay." She turned around to swim away but Will caught her around the waist.

"That's just bullshit. We've never brought any women to the job and fucked them on that table or anywhere else," he told her, his lips wet and smooth against her shoulder.

Leo cupped her cheeks. "What the hell kind of men do you think we are? You want to know the truth? Hell I'll tell you the truth, Adel, I haven't been with a woman sexually for months. That's months, and the reason why is because of you."

She felt her heart race and tears fill her eyes. Was he serious? Was it just a line? She couldn't tell and that frustrated her. Her father, Bentley, the whole situation hurt her so badly she couldn't even tell if Leo was lying or not.

"I'm sorry. God, I'm making a mess of things. I just don't know what to believe. I can't even trust my own gut instincts or feelings. I question everything because of them. Because of what happened.

God, I'm so sorry, I'm so confused." She wanted to pull away but Will hugged her from behind more snuggly.

"Shhh, don't overthink this. Let's just relax and enjoy the day." He kissed her shoulder and Leo cupped her cheek. He looked at her with an expression of sincerity and care.

"We can be friends first. If that's what it takes to gain your trust and for you to see we're the real deal, then so be it."

"Hey, are you guys going to come play or what?" Mercedes called out to them.

"Let's have some fun," Will said and they headed over toward the others to join the game. Her heart was heavy, her mind overloaded with the problems ahead of her, but then she forgot all of them for the time being and enjoyed the day with all her friends, and two new ones, Will and Leo.

* * * *

Leo sat on the blanket next to Will and Adel as the fire burned and the soft sound of a guitar echoed through the evening air. It was a clear, warm, beautiful night. Kurt Dawn strummed the guitar and everyone gathered around.

Steve and his brothers left after they finally seemed to get the hint that they didn't have a chance with Adel. Leo hoped it didn't cause any problems at work, but considering that if all went well, Leo and his brothers would be dating Adel, their personal assistant, a lot of gossip and changes were coming. He felt that uneasy feeling in his gut. They needed to talk to Hank and get him on board. He was resistant to change and to trusting anyone but the two of them. Once they told him about today, and what happened, hopefully he would let that guard down a little and learn to trust.

What really concerned Leo was the guy who was bothering Adel, and who he was and why she hadn't sought out help? Was it an ex-boyfriend? Did he live nearby? Would he come find her and hurt her? He didn't know and the not knowing was driving him crazy.

He glanced at her, absorbed the scent of her shampoo, the fragility and femininity she seemed to emit. It made him feel protective, and if he weren't careful he might say something or do something to offend her or scare her because of this other guy. It was like walking on eggshells but not knowing why. He had to force his thoughts away from that and focus on being with Adel and letting her get used to him and his brothers being close. After all, she wasn't swatting them away or verbally telling them to take a hike. He would take his chances.

He placed his arm behind Adel's shoulders and she leaned back against him. That little show of acceptance brought his arousal higher and damn it his possessive protective meter up a notch. She would be theirs. He was hopeful.

Will placed his hand on her thigh as they sat in front of the fire just listening to music. Some of the others were talking in low voices. Monroe was kissing Alicia's neck as Caldwell held her hand on his lap.

Danny held Marlena on his lap as Mike and Jack spoke softly to Mercedes and Taylor. It was peaceful and one of the reasons why he and his brothers enjoyed living in Chance. These were all good friends. They would do anything for them. He wondered if Adel's friends knew about the guy bothering her or even the sheriff.

His concern for her well-being was making him antsy. He turned toward her as the others started talking about calling it a night. That was fine with him. Some alone time at Adel's place would be perfect.

He leaned closer and kissed her cheek then whispered into her ear.

"Everyone is starting to pack up. We'll give you a ride back to your place, then we can talk some more."

She nodded her head and he winked at Will, who got up then offered a hand to Adel. She took it and when Will pulled her up he wrapped her in his arms and kissed her softly on the lips. It was a quick kiss but at least Adel didn't pull away.

Everyone said good night, and Mercedes asked if Adel was okay with Leo and Will driving her home, and they assured her they would take care of her. As everyone said good-bye and hugged, kissed, talked about doing this again, Leo felt content. These were the kinds of things Will, Leo and Hank wanted to do all the time.

They had been so wrapped up in themselves, and more recently, trying to get Adel out of their heads, that they missed out on some good times with friends. Hopefully this was the beginning of more good times.

"My dress is still damp. Can I give you your shirt back when we get to the cottage?" she asked.

He looked at her wearing his T-shirt and he smiled. It was practically to her knees. "Darling, you can wear my shirt as long as you want to. You look incredible in it." She blushed and shyly looked away as Will took her hand and led her to their truck.

The ride back to her place was short. When they got to her front door she turned around and stopped them.

"I think we should call it a night," she said and lowered her eyes.

He felt disappointed.

"It's still early and we want to talk more," Will told her as he took her hand and caressed her arm, stepping up close to her. He kissed her neck then her shoulder, tickling her. She chuckled and gave him a light shove against his shoulder.

"Just for a little while. To say good night properly," Will added.

She released a small breath and then turned to unlock the front door.

They walked inside and could feel how warm it was in there.

"Damn, baby, it's like a sauna in here."

"I'm sorry, there's no AC in this room, only in the bedroom."

"Oh yeah, I want to see my brother's handiwork," Will said and they walked down the hallway.

"Nice," Will stated as he looked at the ceiling fan. Leo could feel the immediate difference in temperature in this room and the AC was on very low.

She walked over to adjust it.

"Want the fan on, too?" Will asked, reaching for the pull chord.

"Sure, that way it will be nice and cool in here for sleeping tonight."

She went to walk toward the door but Will pulled her close.

"Did you have fun with us today?" he asked.

"Yes, it was a lot of fun."

"Good." He ran his hand along her thigh and then her waist as he leaned down and kissed her softly on the lips. Leo felt his heart racing. She looked so beautiful and he imagined the bikini she wore and how throughout the day he thought about removing it from her body and exploring every inch of her.

Will turned her around so her back was toward Leo as he kissed her.

Leo stepped closer. He hesitated to reach out and touch Adel, afraid to spook her or make her panic. When he finally did and his hands landed gently on her hips, she relaxed. It was as if she waited, anticipated his touch, too.

He leaned forward and kissed her shoulder then as she softened in Will's arms he explored her body with the palm of his hand. He ran it around her waist and in front of her along her belly then up against her breast. She moaned into Will's mouth and Will's hand hit Leo's on her waist then Will stepped back a little and cupped her breast.

Leo ran his hand along her belly again and then lower. He inched his fingers toward where he really wanted to explore and waited for her reaction. Would Adel let him explore her pussy, or was this too much too soon?

"You have an incredible body, baby. This bikini is so sexy, just like you," Leo told her and kissed her neck.

Will deepened the kiss, exploring her mouth and teasing her breast.

"I want to touch you, baby. I want to see how turned on you are having two men kissing you, touching you, and exploring what will be ours soon enough."

He waited for some rejection but instead she pressed closer to Will and then tilted her ass back, giving him room in the front. Leo took it as a sign to advance his fingers lower, and lower he went.

\* \* \* \*

Adel didn't know what came over her, but she was entirely too turned on to not let this go a little farther. She wouldn't sleep with them. She wouldn't do that for quite some time, she couldn't, but the way Will and Leo made her feel was overwhelming. They worked in sync. Will manipulated her breast and nipple as he explored her mouth with his tongue.

The feel of Leo's large, heavy hand caressing over her curves and dipping into her bikini bottoms had her tilting back.

"Oh yeah, open for me, Adel. Show me how badly you want me to stroke your pussy," he whispered and licked her neck then nibbled on a sensitive spot. She moaned and Will released her lips just as Leo pressed a thick, hard finger up into her cunt.

"Oh God. Oh, Leo," she moaned.

"Sweet Jesus you're wet, baby. We're turning you on. You feel it, too, don't you, sweetheart?" Leo asked her and she nodded her head.

"That's good, Adel. We want you to feel safe and comfortable with us. We want to bring you pleasure," Will told her and then lifted her top and explored her breast with his mouth.

She moaned louder as Leo began to stroke faster and then pull out and add a second digit. She was so aroused, so wet and needy she rode his finger. She rocked her hips and let go and just got lost in how perfect they made her feel touching her together.

"Oh God. Oh my," she said, surprised at how good it felt and how stimulated she was.

Will released her breast and then kissed along her belly then to the top of her mound.

"I want to taste you, Adel."

"Oh." She moaned and felt her pussy release some more cream.

"You want that? You'll let my brother and I taste your sweet cream?" Leo asked.

"This is too much."

Leo thrust deeper. "Never too much. You're going to belong to us," Leo stated firmly as Will pressed her bikini bottoms down and Leo sat down on the edge of the bed, causing her legs to part.

Will adjusted them to his liking over Leo's thick hard thighs.

"Just like this, baby. Wide open so I can see what Leo is doing to your pretty wet cunt."

She jerked forward and moaned again.

"I'm going in, bro," Will said and she watched Leo's fingers leave her cunt and then Will leaned forward and licked her pussy lips. He plunged his tongue in deep and then thrust it in and out of her pussy.

She moaned and shook as Leo licked one wet digit and held her gaze. "Delicious," he said and she gushed more cream.

She was oversensitive. Everything rocked her body and made it hum with desire. The way Will's hands held her thighs open, the sight of his forearm muscles, the veins by the side of his temples pulsating as he licked and sucked on her clit harder and harder.

It was all too much and then she felt the wet finger against her mouth and Leo's warm breath against her ear.

"Taste your cream, Adel. See how delicious you are. I need more."

She'd never done anything so brazen, so wild in her life, but Will and Leo brought it out in her as she opened her mouth and licked his thick, hard finger.

He used his other hand to manipulate her breast and then pull on the nipple hard.

"Oh God!" She moaned and she came.

Will suckled and licked at her until Leo complained about getting a taste.

"Oh God, I can't. It's too much."

"Oh no, baby. Never too much. Not when you'll have three lovers like my brothers and me," Leo said and she thought about Hank. Did he really want her, too, or was he just along for the ride? Did she even care if they continued to make her feel like this?

In a flash she was lying on her back on the bed, her legs spread wide, and Leo took Will's place. He slowly pressed a finger to her swollen cunt and she held his gaze.

"You look so fucking sexy. You got my dick really hard, Adel. It's going to be torture not taking you tonight," Leo said and then leaned forward and licked around her pussy lips as he thrust fingers in and out of her cunt.

Will pressed her shirt up and explored her cleavage with his mouth. He licked along the valley and then up to her lips.

"Your pussy is delicious." He plunged his tongue in deeply and explored her mouth, shocking her into acquiescence.

She felt her body tighten up and then explode again. The sounds of Leo slurping her cream aroused her even further and she knew if they just pushed a little more she would let them fuck her. What did she have to lose? She wasn't a virgin. She knew what men wanted and she already had her heart broken, but deep inside she knew that wasn't her. She wanted more. She desired love, compassion, true feelings, and a man she could trust. This was chemistry, lust, and nothing more. She accepted that as she kissed Will back until Leo pulled her bikini bottoms back up into place and Will released her lips.

Leo joined them on the bed and she cuddled between them.

Leo caressed along her belly and Will cupped her breast.

"Thank you for trusting us tonight. It's a first step in the right direction, baby. You'll see, everything will work out just fine," Leo told her and then he kissed her softly.

Will smiled and Adel closed her eyes and relished in the rest of the time they would spend together tonight. Tomorrow she would deal with the consequences of letting her guard down, when trouble was breathing down her throat.

# Chapter 3

Hank sat next to Adel in the meeting room going over the specs on the job and trying to decipher how they would go about planning a schedule and breaking everything down. He knew about the weekend and how things had gone down by the lake and back at her cottage with his brothers. Hank would be lying to himself if he said he didn't care and wasn't interested, but he really didn't know Adel and he didn't do relationships well at all. She was sweet, and even his parents liked her which was a first, but he was concerned. She could be after something. She could just want their money because she was poor. It was a fact.

Her cottage was one of the smallest in that neighborhood. She didn't have a job until his father hired her here and talked them into taking the personal assistant position that had come up. He wasn't sure about her, other than she was strikingly good-looking, had a killer body, and was sweet as could be. In fact, he felt badly if he made a flirtatious comment or insulted her. He felt different when it came to Adel. He acted differently.

The thought sounded so snotty and that wasn't him, but he conditioned himself to believe that no one was good enough, trustworthy enough for him to open his heart to. Inhaling Adel's perfume, hearing her thoughts and knowledge on construction, and sitting this close to her was breaking down the walls he put up so well. She had some sort of guy bothering her, however, and he worried about what trouble she might bring his brothers. He didn't mince words or beat around the bush so he took it upon himself to find out what was going on.

"So, I heard that you had an enjoyable time by the lake this weekend. I wish I could have made it but I had a prior engagement to attend."

Her cheeks turned a nice shade of red and he couldn't help but to glance at her breasts she hid fairly well behind the blouse she wore with her skirt today.

"It was fun. Everyone had a good time," she added as she looked up from the paper, her pen in hand. She was petite, feminine, and so beautiful he felt his heartbeat increase. From what Leo and Will told him, she was very responsive to their touches and being aroused by two men.

"I heard. I guess I missed all the fun, but maybe next time, right?" he asked and she nodded her head.

He looked at her lips and then into her eyes.

"My brothers told me all about it. I have some concerns," he said and she looked worried.

"They mentioned some guy bothering you, and calling you. Would you like to tell me who he is and what he's after?"

"No," she said and looked away from him.

He was shocked at her response. Usually when he asked her to do something she did it. What was she hiding?

"Why not? It sounds like trouble and if you're in some kind of trouble my brothers and I can help you."

"I don't need any help. I told Leo and Will that."

He slid his arm along the back of her chair. She was being stubborn and their concern seemed justified.

"Is it some ex-boyfriend? Does he want you back?"

She swung her head around to look him in the eyes. He nailed it. That was easy.

"It's none of your business Hank, just like it's none of Will's or Leo's. Just leave it alone."

"But my brothers are worried. I'm worried," he added when she looked at him like he was a jerk.

"There's no need to be. I can take care of myself."

He couldn't resist. He caressed her shoulder and leaned closer.

"But we can take care of you."

"You? I'm not doing this," she stated and stood up from her chair. He followed, towering over her by more than a foot.

"You're not doing what?"

"Having this conversation with my boss."

"Oh I think I'm more than that," he replied sarcastically.

She placed her hands on her hips.

"Really? How is that? Because last I checked I was hanging out with Will and Leo, not you." She went to walk away and something came over him. A possessiveness, a desire to kiss her, touch her, and be part of what his brothers and her shared. He grabbed her upper arm to stop her.

"I'm sorry I wasn't there. Plans were made."

"With who?" she asked, seeming angry and it hit him. She was jealous. She thought he was with another woman. He smiled softly. "I wasn't with another woman."

She looked embarrassed and lowered her head a moment.

"That's none of my business if you were or weren't."

"Do you want it to be?" he asked, pressing closer.

"What do you mean?"

"I mean, do you care to know? Does the thought of me being with another woman make you jealous?"

Her eyes widened and he quickly added, "Because the thought of you with another man other than Leo and Will makes me really angry. Haven't you noticed my reaction when Steve or even Levi talks to you and touches you? It makes me crazy. So don't think for one moment that I purposely didn't go to the lake with my brothers. I'm a busy man and plans were made beforehand."

She held his gaze, those doe eyes of hers slowly pushing against the wall around his heart.

"I'm not some item to be passed around between the three of you. Leo, Will, and I shared a lot the other night."

"I heard what you all shared," he told her and then looked at her lips.

"I also know that you were scared, hesitant to start something between all of us. Friends first, I think Leo said. But you see, I'm not good at slow, or at making friends. When I want something I go after it. Some people can handle that and others can't," he challenged.

"How about you, Adel?"

"You don't intimidate me," she replied, her voice cracking.

He reached up and cupped her cheek as he held her gaze. "I should intimidate you. I don't trust easily. I don't date. I don't play games. I also expect an answer, the truth when I ask a question." He caressed her lower lip and leaned closer.

He stared into those big brown eyes of hers and knew he had complete control, but instead of making him feel triumphant, he felt like a dick for scaring her. What was she afraid of? Why did he have such different, deep emotions for a woman he hardly knew? Before he could say anything more the door opened. He released her and Leo was there with a smile on his face.

"Sorry I'm late," he said.

"That's okay, I need to take some pictures of these designs and then enter them into the computer," Adel said and took out her cell phone, took a few pictures, then gasped as Leo wrapped an arm around her waist from behind and kissed her neck.

"I missed you, baby," he said and she looked worried.

"Leo, I thought we talked about this. I don't want people talking. I want things to be normal around here," she told him.

"Normal? That's not happening. You and I will talk more later," Hank told her and Leo gave him a hard expression.

* * * *

Adel was feeling out of sorts and very on edge with her emotions. The past several days Hank would hint at wanting her, or come close to touching her, even kissing her, and then hold back. She started to feel desperate to have him kiss her, especially since Leo and Will took every opportunity they had to touch her, kiss her, and even tell her how badly they wanted to visit her cottage again to check on the ceiling fan. They were such flirts, but Hank was reserved and hard. It scared her yet made her want to break him down. Which was crazy because she should be running from these three men, not wanting them.

She snuck out of the office early for lunch wanting to avoid having lunch with Leo or Will so she could talk to Mercedes. She was feeling crazy and needed some good advice. She met up with her by the deli and they ordered lunch then took it to the park to eat.

"Oh God, Hank is totally the silent brooding type. You have it bad, girl," Mercedes teased her.

"I think I'm setting myself up for more rejection and pain. Why would a man like him and his brothers be interested in a woman like me? I mean I have nothing. I come from a wealthy family that basically rejected me because of my ex. My mom is hounding me to come visit and making me feel guilty because my dad's been sick. Never mind the annoying phone calls from my ex."

"You should talk to Max about your ex bothering you. What if he shows up here and hurts you?"

"He likes to make threats and he thinks he still has a hold of me somehow even though I broke off the engagement and left my family. I looked up information on the company and he's taken over the majority of the shares. He's pushing my dad out and that was what my dad sold me out for."

"Then that serves your dad right. He chose a business deal over his own daughter. That's fucked up big time."

"Yeah, well I doubt he's learned his lesson even though my mom says he has and wants to make amends with me. It's so frustrating,

Mercedes, because I think he's the reason why I'm holding back with Leo, Will, and even Hank. I'm afraid of them rejecting me once I give them my trust, never mind sleep with them. That's intimate and as close as a couple can get. Three men and me making love? I would never be the same again. It will kill me when they leave me. So why bother?" Adel said as the tear escaped her eyes. She quickly wiped it and Mercedes wrapped her arm around Adel's shoulder.

"Sweetie, they really did a number on you, but I think you've tortured yourself enough. Why not take a chance with Leo, Will, and Hank? They could turn out to be the best thing that ever happened to you, but you won't know if you don't take this chance."

"But I'm scared, and I don't want to tell them about my ex and about my dad because if they really aren't as wonderful as they seem then they could use that against me and know how vulnerable I am."

"They're not your ex and certainly not your father."

"We don't know that."

"Honey, they like you a lot, and you like them a lot. Just enjoy their company and see where it leads. Take your time and see what happens. If you follow your heart and your gut it will be just fine."

"That's a problem, too. What my dad did to me, choosing Bentley and the business deal over me, killed me. Then to know that my dad knew Bentley was cheating on me with multiple women and that he still wanted me to marry Bentley is sick. It makes me wonder if my dad has been faithful to my mom all these years. I mean she's hounding me to come home to visit and even after all this crap I feel guilty and want to cut the ties and end it all. Do I go and try to make amends and then tell my dad we don't have to ever discuss it again, or do I just go on feeling guilty for not trying? It's a mess."

"I can't tell you what to do. You're a good person. That's why you feel guilty even though you shouldn't. Hold off telling the guys about your dad and Bentley for now. You'll know when the time is right to tell them. Follow your heart. They'll make you happy and you don't have to deal with Bentley or your mom and dad again."

Adel and Mercedes finished up lunch and then Adel headed back to the office. She wasn't sure what to do and on her way through town she saw Harold Ferguson. He smiled wide and hugged her hello. How badly she wished she had a dad like Harold or like his brother William.

"Hello, Mr. Ferguson, how are you?"

"Adel, how many times have I told you to call me Harold?"

She smiled and then stepped back. "Okay, but it's hard to do."

"Well, how is my future daughter-in-law doing today?" he asked and she felt her mouth drop and her face turned bright red.

Harold laughed and then looped his arm through hers and walked her in the opposite direction of the company.

"Now, don't be embarrassed, gossip travels fast around Chance and of course the fact that my three sons who I thought might never settle down started threatening men."

"What?" she asked and he explained about Hank, Leo, and Will telling guys that liked her to stay clear that she belonged to them. She didn't know if she should be touched or angry.

"But I'm not involved with them."

Harold raised one of his eyebrows up at her in challenge.

"Well, I mean not officially. They haven't taken me out on a date, and, Hank is just, complicated."

He chuckled.

"You have flustered my son Hank so much he doesn't know which way is up and which is down. I was just in there and he was in a pissed off mood. Heard from Will that Hank hasn't kissed you yet or made his desire to make you his woman official."

"Oh God, you guys have such a great relationship that they tell you this stuff. It's so weird," she said then exhaled. Harold laughed.

"Not weird. Special. My brother William and I along with Ethena have raised our sons to be able to talk to us about anything and not feel embarrassed, uncomfortable, or afraid. Believe me, the kind of trouble those three young men got into when they were younger gave me some of my gray hairs in my early thirties." She laughed and then she felt sad.

He stopped, turned her toward him, and looked down into her eyes.

"You're scared, aren't you?"

She nodded her head.

He took a deep breath and released it. He seemed angry and she knew why. Harold knew what her dad and Bentley had done to her. He knew about her family and even her mom, who he felt badly for.

"Come on, let's sit and talk this out."

"But work."

"I still own a share or few more than my sons so no worries," he teased.

They took a seat on the bench and they talked about the situation.

He got very serious.

"Adel, Bentley is a dangerous man. He's hurt you before. I know he hit you, was physically and verbally abusive. You need to report this. We should see Max."

She shook her head. "I don't want anyone to know about what happened to me. It's embarrassing," she said and felt the tears in her eyes. Then she felt Harold's hand cover hers and she looked up into his eyes. He was sad, too.

"If he continues to bother you, you'll need to confide in Max. As the sheriff he'll make sure to keep it on the down low, but you should confide in my sons. They care for you a lot already."

"How do you know they do? How do you know I'm not just something for now like the others?" she asked.

"Well first of all, if they are then they'll get my boot up their asses one after the next." She giggled.

"Seriously, I know my sons. I've never seen them react to a woman the way they instantly and separately reacted to you since day one. You've proven your capabilities, your knowledge of the construction business, and that puts you on a higher level than most, both female and male. You've covered for them and their indiscretions, which I'm sure has given you reservations about trust. Believe me, they're kicking themselves in the ass for trying to act like morons. You've been professional and kind to them but ultimately it's the equally shared attraction to you."

She looked away and shook her head.

"I'm so confused right now. I feel like I'm just starting to get control of my life and make decisions on my own for the first time. Despite Bentley calling me and texting me frequently, I still feel like I'm surviving on my own and if I give into this attraction or whatever, that I'm setting myself up for more heartache."

"That's understandable, Adel. Bentley and your dad hurt you. That's not easy to get over. Will my sons hurt you, too? I don't believe they would. Besides, no one is saying by exploring this attraction to them that you're giving up control or power, or your newfound independence. If anything, I think your independence, your work ethics and truthfulness are all things people find likable and are impressed with. Take your time and see where it leads, but you must promise me that you'll come to me if there's any trouble. I mean with my sons, with Bentley, or your father, with anything. I want you to know that I'm here for you, so never feel alone."

He smiled at her and Adel felt the tears fill her eyes. She was all choked up and couldn't even say thank you. It seemed she didn't have to. He patted her knee and stood up.

"Shall we head back to work? I want to get an update on this new project you all have been working on."

"You mean your sons haven't been filling you in?"

"Well, maybe a little here and there." He winked, and Adel knew that Harold stayed on top of things with the company even though he gave complete operations and control over to his sons.

They headed inside and she was feeling a little bit better after the encouragement from both Harold and Mercedes. Then she locked gazes with Hank as she entered the door. He looked pissed off. What else was new? That was Hank's expression most of the time.

Harold guided her inside, saying hello to some employees as she made her way past Hank. He stopped her, touching her hand. She looked up into his eyes. He towered over her despite the heels she wore.

"Are you okay?" he whispered, his voice, that tone affecting her instantly. She nodded.

"I'm good. I'll meet you in the meeting room shortly."

"I saw you talking with my dad, and you disappeared for lunch, not even telling us where you went. Are you sure that you're okay?" he asked and she could sense his sincerity. Hell, even with her emotions screwed up and her guard on high alert all the time, she sensed his care.

"I'm good. You have a great father. You're lucky to have him," she said.

He released her hand, looked perplexed at her comment, and then she headed inside, but not before noticing Levi Holmes watching her. She looked away, but the hairs on the back of her neck stood up and an uneasy feeling filled her belly. She didn't like that guy. He was definitely creepy.

# Chapter 4

"I don't know about this," Will stated with his arms crossed as he stood in front of Hank's desk. Leo was smirking.

"Why not? It's a good opportunity for Hank to get to know Adel on a more personal level, and to schmooze with the Morrisons. You'll need as much help as you can get to impress their project manager, Cadence Crowe. What a douche bag that guy is," Leo added.

"You're not kidding. Thanks to Dad we found out about this dinner party and got the invite for the fundraiser. I'd better go ask her now to be sure she has enough time to get ready," Hank said and then cleared his throat and fixed the tie he wore with his dress shirt today.

"Go get her, brother," Will teased and Hank gave him a dirty look.

His brothers, the little wise-ass bastards, knew that Adel made him nervous. Those nerves came across in orders and barks at everyone including Adel.

He walked out of the office and saw her on the phone. She was writing something down on a pad of paper and stating that she would check Leo's calendar to see if he were available for a dinner. He wondered who it was and as she disconnected the call she looked sad. His stomach churned. What had gotten her upset?

"Adel?" he said her name as he approached her desk. She turned to look at him and it seemed she had tears in her eyes.

"What's wrong?" he asked.

"Nothing," she replied and looked him over. She had complimented his tie the other day but had yet to make any compliment today. Maybe she didn't like green ties. He would have to note that. What was he thinking? She didn't even say she didn't like it.

"Hank, is there something you needed?" she asked, interrupting his own idiotic mental conversation.

"Oh, um, I need your assistance with something for tomorrow night. There's a dinner, a fundraising event in Lancaster. The Morrisons are going to be there and I was wondering. Well, if you weren't busy, or had any plans, that perhaps you could go with me? As my date?"

"A date, but also business?"

"Well…yes, but a good opportunity for the two of us to spend some alone time together. Well, I mean not completely alone because we're going to a party but, you know what I mean."

She smiled at him and it seemed like she was laughing at him. She made him so damn nervous, he acted like a virgin. Fuck, where did that thought come from? Hell, she was gorgeous and had a sexy body of course he would love to explore it.

"I guess I can change my plans. I was just meeting the girls for a movie night. Oh, what is the dress code? Fancy, cocktail dress, gown? I don't have a lot of things in my wardrobe," she said and then lowered her eyes as if she were embarrassed for not having a gazillion outfits.

"Surely, you would look stunning in anything. I would say cocktail dress most likely. It's at a small venue. Invite only. I can pick you up at your place at seven? Will that work for tomorrow night?"

"Sure."

"Great."

He stood there watching her, unable to take his eyes off of her. Her big brown doe eyes held his, the thick lashes accentuating them even more so, and the conservative pale pink outfit hugged her figure. He wanted to ask her to get him some coffee or bend over and look in the filing cabinet for a file just to see her walk, her hips sway, and the roundness of her ass.

He cleared his throat, smiled, then turned around and headed back into his office. His brothers were there to tease him.

"See, she accepted. Now make sure this dinner is not just business. Make sure to talk to her and ask questions, get to know her," Leo told him.

"Yeah, and seal it with a kiss. You'll never be the same again. I'm not," Will said as he glanced out through the cracked doorway.

"Oh brother. I've been on dates before and on business ones, too. I'll handle it fine."

"No, Hank, this is different. Adel is special. Remember that. We want her to be our woman. She can complete us. Don't fuck this up."

Hank gulped and he felt the pressure was on. How the hell would he not screw this up when Adel made him so damn nervous?

* * * *

Adel wasn't certain about the dress but Mercedes, Marlena, and Alicia all told her she looked stunning in it and sexy as well as sophisticated. The dress was a cream, almost golden, color that hugged her figure to right above the knee. The classy bodice came up in spaghetti straps and the low dip accentuated her cleavage but didn't appear overwhelming. She wore a small gold heart covered in diamonds that was fake but looked real. She'd fallen in love with it and wished she could afford one with real diamonds, but that was a wish that would take time to achieve.

She looked at herself in the full-length mirror, glad she found the high-heeled shoes that matched the color of the dress perfectly. With her tan skin, she looked amazing, and felt amazing. It was funny how putting on makeup, dressing up in a pretty dress with high heels made life seem better and happier even for just an evening.

The doorbell rang and she suddenly felt sick to her stomach.

What would Hank think of her dress? Would he find her beautiful and sexy or think she wasn't quite as lovely as most women he dated?

The lack of self-confidence hit her hard as she headed to the front door.

This was it, either the night would be successful and fun or a total mess.

As she opened the door she felt her heart race and pound inside of her chest. Hank looked incredibly handsome. He had on a red bowtie with a black dress shirt, black pants, black dress shoes, and a bouquet of wild flowers.

"Adel, you look stunning," he told her and then leaned forward to kiss her cheek. He stepped back, handed her the flowers, and she welcomed him into her home.

She got a vase, added water, and arranged the bouquet.

\* \* \* \*

"This is a nice place you have here. So clean and beautifully decorated."

"Oh, thank you. It's small but it's perfect for me."

"Is it different from the last place you lived before moving to Chance?" he asked, coming closer to the counter in the small kitchen. He could smell her enticing perfume and his eyes roamed over her body in appreciation. Adel looked classy, sexy, and stunning all in one.

"I lived in a big house with my parents." She got quiet as she came closer, grabbing her small purse off the counter.

"I like this a lot better. All set?" she asked him.

"Sure thing." They headed out the door and she locked it as they left. He opened the car door to the Range Rover to let her in then hurried around to the front.

"This is a nice car. I always wondered what it looked like inside."

"Why didn't you ask me? I would have shown you, even given you a ride," he said, looking over her body and the fact she sat in his car as his date. He was excited. He had high hopes for this evening, both business and personal.

He shifted the gear and took off down the dirt road as he made small talk with Adel. There was a lot riding on this date, including getting to know the woman his brothers were positive was the one. He on the other hand had his reservations. Why? Because he was a hardened soul. He didn't trust easy. It had to be earned and even then he truly didn't trust just anyone and certainly never a woman he planned on getting intimate with. That thought made him clear his throat. He hadn't even gotten to first base and he was assuming a celebratory home run.

"So, what's the game plan? Do we avoid talking with the Morrisons involving business or what?" she asked him.

He glanced at her legs. They were crossed and looking tan, toned, and sexy as she sat in the passenger seat. By now on the few dates he had over the years, the woman would be touching him or at minimum his hand would be between her legs.

He really worked hard at keeping women out of his heart and wanted nothing more than pleasurable sex when needed. When he looked at Adel, it made him feel like a jerk, but also wonder how experienced she was.

"I say let the conversation flow freely. My family has known the Morrisons for years and we don't want to come across as badgering them to accept nor do we want to come across as if we don't care either way."

"I understand. So how come Leo and Will didn't come along, too?"

He looked at her as he got onto the highway. Just a few exits and they would be there.

"I wanted to spend a little time with you alone so we could get to know one another."

She clasped her hands and looked away from him. It made him feel like she wasn't interested in him, only Will and Leo.

"Is that okay with you, or are you only interested in my brothers and not me?"

She swung her head toward him. "You're my bosses and I don't know if getting involved with all of you is such a great idea."

He focused on the road, glancing at her in hopes of showing his sincerity.

"Adel, I'm not going to lie to you and tell you that I'm ready to jump right into this. I'm not. I have my reservations, my concerns, but, that's part of why I asked you out tonight. Consider this a date, and a time for us to get to know one another. No pressure on either end. I just want to get to know you outside of work, aside from being my personal assistant. Since you said yes to coming with me, I assume you want that, too, and to get to know me?"

He waited for her response and hoped that she indeed wanted to get to know him. This was crazy.

"I do." He smiled and reached over to cover her hands with his. The difference in size was amazing.

"Thank you. So tell me about this family of yours and the house you lived in. Was it in South Carolina?"

She looked shocked and he felt her hands tense up. He squinted his eyes but focused on the road.

"Too personal?" he asked.

She swallowed hard. He heard her.

"It's not far from Chance. Maybe an hour. It was a big house on a large estate in a nice neighborhood. I like the small towns better. People are nicer to one another, to their neighbors, and not worried about impressing one another."

He chuckled.

"That's true. I like smaller towns, too, although my Aunt Betsey would say a bit of competition is a good thing to keep people on their toes and not looking like slobs."

She laughed as he made the turn off the exit and then slowly approached the venue.

"Well, here we are."

There was a valet to take their car since parking was limited.

Hank noticed the way the young guys looked at Adel as the car attendant opened her car door and then took her hand to assist her. That really wasn't necessary and it pissed Hank off.

He met her in the front of the vehicle as he took the card number from the kid and then placed his hand at the dip in Adel's lower back.

"Are you okay?" she whispered.

"Fine," he said in a hard tone as another person opened the door for them to enter.

One glance around the room and he could tell this was going to be an interesting party.

"Hank, oh my goodness, how wonderful to see you."

He heard the voice and knew it was Collette. The tall, thin blonde was decked out in her designer wear and holding a glass of champagne.

"Collette, so nice to see you."

"Hm, I bet. You lose my number, Hank? Why, who is this pretty little angel?" she asked and one look at Adel and she seemed to read right through Collette's tactics. Hank never should have slept with the snob. She thought she was someone of importance.

"This is Adel McKinley."

"Adel? Oh, you mean your secretary?" Collette asked and then placed her palm against Hank's chest and whispered into his ear.

"You poor darling. Resorting to a female employee for a business date? You should have called me. I would have made it worth your while."

She walked away and he shook his head. Adel looked insulted so he quickly grabbed her hand and headed toward the crowd of people.

"Sorry about that."

"You are, or should I expect some more ex-lovers to approach us as the evening goes on? Maybe let me know if you'd like to introduce me as your personal assistant or your date?" she snapped at him and he was shocked, but also entirely turned on. He pressed her hip closer to him and gave her hip a squeeze. Just as he was about to tell her what her firmness did to his cock, Michelle Morrison along with Credence Crowe approached.

"Hank, good to see you. I didn't know you were coming tonight. And who is this beautiful young woman?" Michelle Morrison asked, and as he answered he saw Credence Crowe look her over and give a smile.

"This is Adel, we work together."

"Oh, how interesting. Well, do tell me how your family is doing? I thought for sure Harold and William would have attended. I haven't seen Ethena in months."

"Well they had a previous engagement to attend, or I'm certain they would be here," he told her as Credence shook Adel's hand hello and moved closer to her.

"Well, this is an important event, and we've received wonderful donations to bid on. Why don't I show you," she suggested and he didn't want to insult the woman and certainly not leave Adel either.

"Adel?" He motioned with his hand for her to follow.

"Oh, don't worry, Hank, I'll keep Adel company while Michelle gets you to open your wallet for a great cause."

He looked at Adel and she smiled and nodded her head, indicating she was okay with this. However, as Hank followed Michelle, with her arm looped through his, he couldn't help but look over his shoulder at Adel and Credence. Credence placed his hand at her lower back and guided her toward the champagne table.

\* \* \* \*

In all of about five minutes Adel saw right through Credence and his façade. She had dealt with men like him for years and being around Bentley. As Credence dropped flirtatious comments and hinted for information on whether she was dating Hank, she played it off as them being friends first and that she didn't think it was a good idea about getting involved with her boss. After all, part of this date was doing recon on the Morrisons and where they stood in the bidding war for the job.

"I think that's very wise of you. I must tell you that I don't know Hank or his brothers well, but only what I've heard through the gossip," he told her seriously.

"Well, don't believe everything you hear. They are very smart, resourceful, and professional men. Their business comes before everything and they're committed to any projects they take on. In fact, they get most of their jobs from word of mouth."

He smiled softly.

"Is that so? No advertising, or greasing any palms?" he said.

She scrunched her eyebrows together and gave him an angry expression. "Mr. Crowe, I don't know what kind of business Morrison's company is that you work for, but I can tell you that Ferguson construction is on the up and up. No greasing any palms or funny games and promises. That's what I like about working for them. They are a major part of Chance, and help support the community they live in with providing jobs to those in need and have been known to make up positions in the company to help someone who is down and out. I don't believe men like that run any shady scams or dirty business."

She looked away from him and toward Hank, who was still talking with Michelle and a few other people. She felt Credence's hand on her waist then his breath against her ear as he whispered, "The Ferguson men are very lucky men to have you. So loyal and supportive. Perhaps you could fill me in more?"

"How so?" she asked cautiously.

"Well, my bosses, JT and JR, are very interested in in accepting whatever bid Ferguson construction submits on the job we're in charge of, but they are a bit smaller than one of the other construction companies that recently inquired about the job."

"Who would that be?" she asked, hoping to get a little upper hand.

"Oh, I'm not at liberty to say right now, but how involved have you been in the preparing of their proposal if I may ask?"

"Very involved. I have a lot of insight into jobs of this standard and size. Hank, Will, and Leo have wonderful ideas and a way of working a construction site that is safe and productive."

She went on to tell him about an incident she witnessed where someone didn't take the safety measures required by Ferguson construction and how workers were hurt. She explained about Hank firing the workers who were cutting corners and not taking the rules seriously.

He seemed impressed and as they talked about the job she gave some feedback and just enough information on ideas to plant a seed that Ferguson construction was more than capable of handling this job for Morrison.

She glanced toward Hank's direction and saw two other young women talking to him. He was chatting back and forth with them and the women were touching his arm or hugging it. It appeared as if they were vying for his attention. She was shocked at the feeling of jealousy she felt.

"Adel, I would like you to meet my bosses, JT and JR Morrison. This is Adel McKinley. She's the personal assistant for Hank and his brothers.

She smiled as she shook their hands hello. They were strikingly handsome men. Tall, dark, and eyes the deepest blue she had ever seen.

"Such a pleasure to meet you, Adel. Are Hank, Will, and Leo here, too?" JT asked, looking around. She took a peek over her shoulder and saw Hank still speaking with the women and appearing quite enthralled in the conversation.

"He's right over there near your mom. I just met her a short time ago. This is quite the fundraising event."

"Yes it is," JR said to her then Credence stopped the waiter walking around with champagne. He offered her some and she accepted the glass from him as Credence passed them around.

"Have you worked for the Ferguson brothers long?" JT asked her as his eyes zeroed in on her breasts then her lips and eyes.

"A little over a year." She felt a little uncomfortable standing here with three men she didn't know and each so good-looking and charismatic, but her date was not coming back so quickly so she might as well find out who these men were.

The longer they talked the more she realized that they were very nice men and very professional. They took pride in the family business so she pointed out how Ferguson construction was a family business and how she was friends with Harold and he got her the job with the company.

"How is it working for those three? I hear that Hank went through a handful of personal assistants," Credence said and she wondered if he were trying to steer her clear of getting into a personal relationship with Hank. He seemed to have a bit of an attitude when it came to Hank. Maybe he was just jealous.

"She must be amazing because she's lasted the longest," JR added before she could respond.

"He's a hard one to work with from what I've heard. Not very personable," Credence added, and JT and JR mumbled a reply that seemed unsure.

"From what I've learned over the year working for Hank is that he takes the business and his family's well-being as priority and his responsibility. That being said, there's a lot of pressure when you're the one taking the hits, the negatives and positives as the fall guy. You gentleman probably understand that and feel that way sometimes, too, considering this was your father's company. It's something to be proud of, and I think Hank has accomplished that. With the help of Leo and Will of course, but that's just my observation as a personal assistant," she said then took a sip of champagne.

"Hello, JT, JR. Thank you, Credence, for keeping Adel company while I was held up," Hank said, joining them and keeping a hand at Adel's lower back. The men smiled.

"Are you kidding? The pleasure was all ours. Adel was just talking about the company and her position there. I'd say she's a good one to hold on to," JT said to him.

Hank smiled and Adel wondered if he would be angry that she spoke about the company and him.

"Yeah, don't go making her angry and firing her. We've heard personal assistants don't last long around you," Credence teased.

"Well if he were foolish enough to do so, which I'm certain he isn't, Credence, then I'd hire her on the spot. It's not easy finding hardworking employees who are loyal to their bosses and the business," JR added and winked at Adel.

She smiled and lowered her eyes.

"On another business note, how is the estimate and bid coming along for the job in Langley? I hope you'll make the deadline in time," JR asked.

"We've been diligently working on it. My brothers and I want to make sure that we have everything correct. Adel's been a huge help," Hank said and nudged her shoulder. It was supposed to be brotherly but it felt completely arousing to her.

"Well, Adel, if you have any questions before the final submission you call me directly. I'd be happy to answer any questions you have or even meet up," Credence said as he held her gaze. She knew as well as the other men in the circle what Credence was doing. Hitting on her and trying to get a rile out of Hank. She needed to make sure Hank knew Credence's game. She hugged Hank's arm and felt the tension in it.

"I doubt that would be necessary, Credence. After all, as I was saying earlier, Hank and his brothers are very thorough and cover all their bases, but I'll keep your offer in mind."

Credence nodded his head. Hank's body tightened even more.

The men excused themselves and Hank took her hand and walked her toward the large banquet tables adorned with food and ice sculptures. There were different types of imported cheese and fruits as well as carved meats, fresh breads, and an array of desserts. Along the wall were coffee and latte stations, cordials, after-dinner drinks of all kinds and a wide variety of other desserts.

"This is impressive," she whispered to Hank. His fingers gripped her hand tighter. She looked up, locking gazes with his deep blue eyes as he licked his lower lip and stared at her deeply.

"You're way more appetizing then anything here. Anything I've ever come across."

She swallowed slowly.

"That's quite the line, Hank," she replied, feeling on the defensive and completely knocked off balance by him. His words, those eyes, and that deep, intense stare of his did a number on her body. She went to move and he gripped her hips as he pressed up against her back.

He whispered into her ear, "That wasn't a line. It was the truth."

"Are you sure you didn't use it earlier on the women swarming around you?" she asked, letting the fact that she felt jealous earlier out in the open.

"Not a chance. Perhaps you were laying your own lines down on the Morrisons and Credence, considering all three of them couldn't take their eyes off of you." He gripped her hips tighter and her whole body was on fire.

"Maybe we should eat something before we head out. Come on. I want to be alone with you," he whispered then kissed her ear.

She was shaking she was so aroused and excited about being alone with Hank. The chemistry was definitely there, and also the possessiveness.

He guided her along the way, each of them taking a few things to eat. They found a spot to sit by a small table and enjoyed some of the food, but when he brushed a thumb along her lower lip, claiming she had something there right before he kissed it away, she knew they needed to go, or her legs might not hold her up. She felt needy.

* * * *

Hank tried to slow his pace as they exited the affair that was way too crowded. He just wanted to get Adel into the dark parking lot by his car. He wanted to kiss her, touch her, hold her in his arms and relish in the fact that she was going home with him and not some other man wanting her at this party. She was stunning, smart, and loyal.

"Ah, hell, baby," he said as they got to the Ranger Rover parked in the dark. He pulled her into his arms and kissed her deeply. The feel of her delicate hands rubbing along his back as he devoured her moans excited him more. He gripped her thigh and brought it up high against his thigh.

He released her lips, nibbling along her jaw and then her neck.

"You're so beautiful, Adel," he told her, his cock hard beneath his dress pants, his breathing growing rapider by the second. He wanted her. He wanted to lift her dress, rip off her panties, and fuck her so hard, so deep he got lost in her perfection.

He tore his mouth away from her as he battled against what was right and what needed to be done. He couldn't treat her like all the other women he had met in his life. She was different. She was sweet, pure, perfect, and his brothers were right, Adel would complete them.

He stepped back and gripped her arm.

"Get in the car." She slid onto the seat and she looked at him with those sweet, doe eyes and he nearly faltered. He couldn't take her like this and without his brothers. What happened tonight just solidified the fact that she was going to be theirs. All of theirs.

He got into the driver's side.

"Hank?"

"No questions. Give me a minute. There's too much in my head," he said and she turned away. He felt like a dick but he was losing his mind. It was like he was worthless, a mean son of a bitch all this time, and she was too good for him. Wasn't that crazy? He was the one that turned every woman away and claimed they weren't good enough for him. They were nothing in comparison to Adel. She was perfect.

As he sped down the roadway he felt her hand touch his leg. He tensed up.

"Hank, what's wrong? What did I do that you're angry with me?"

He didn't respond right away.

"I didn't like you flirting with Credence or with the Morrisons."

"I wasn't flirting with them. They asked me questions, and I responded."

"That's not what it looked like," he replied.

He drove a little faster.

"Besides, I could say the same about you. You left me with Credence. You remained over at the tables with those women. They were touching your arm and hugging you and you did nothing to keep them off. Credence, JT, and JR didn't touch me," she replied.

"He had his hand on your lower back."

"She was hugging, hugging your arm. Big difference," she replied and he gripped the steering wheel tighter.

It wasn't until he got to the main entrance of his house, the one he shared with Will and Leo, that he realized he was taking her home.

She didn't seem to notice until the car came to a complete stop. He usually parked in the garage, but instead he parked right outside of the front entrance to their home.

"For the record, I didn't like them doing that to me but I couldn't exactly push them off. It could be misconstrued as being handsy." He opened the car door then slammed it closed. Before he made it around the passenger side she was out of the car.

"That is such a lame excuse. I've heard it all, Hank. I get what tonight was about. It was about schmoozing the Morrisons and winning over Credence, the project manager. Would it have helped seal the deal if I slept with him?" she asked.

That was it. Hank lost it.

He pulled her close, lifted her up against his chest, and kissed her. Their hands were all over one another. He pressed her against the Range Rover and thrust his cock against her mound. She moaned into his mouth and tugged on his hair, fighting for control of the kiss. He ran his hands up her dress, pulled on her panties, maneuvering them and his hands, thrusting his fingers up into her cunt.

She cried out, tearing her mouth from his and giving him full access to her neck and her breasts. He nipped her mouth and she thrust back against him.

"Look at me," he demanded. His fingers continued to thrust up into her wet pussy and he wanted more. He wanted all of her orgasms.

"Credence can never have what's mine and my brothers. Never."

He kissed her deeply and she shook as she came in his arms.

"What in God's name is going on?" Lee asked as he and Leo came outside only wearing jeans.

Adel tried catching her breath as he pulled her away from the Rover and headed toward them.

"Adel is going to officially become all ours tonight. No other man can ever have her but the three of us," Hank announced.

He waited for her protest, for her to deny what was happening between them, but it never came. Instead she laid her head against his shoulder and softly kissed the skin on his neck as Hank carried her into the house and to the main bedroom.

* * * *

Adel was shaking. She thought about all the things that could go wrong here. They could be using her. Not one, not two, but three sexy, wealthy, gorgeous men who had their choice of any woman they wanted to seduce. That scared her.

Two, she could lose her job, the only income she had, and be forced to leave Chance from embarrassment and head back home to sulk and be told that she never should have left Bentley.

Three, she could get her heart completely broken because even though she fought so hard to not let these three men into her heart, especially Hank, she did anyway. She stuck up for him, she praised them, and she was going to have sex with them.

Hank set her feet down on the thick, soft rug. She barely paid attention to her surroundings, but could tell that these men enjoyed the regular things in life, not the extravagant or showy stuff.

The room was done in earth tones with deep beige on the upper walls, a dark brown on the lower walls, with crown molding as a trail rail along the center separating the two colors. The bed was huge, with a thick beige comforter and a bunch of different shades of brown pillows plus a few unique ones with deer heads embroidered on them. It was masculine and sexy like the three of them.

Hank caressed her arms and looked down into her eyes.

"What happened?" Leo asked, moving closer and taking in the sight of her. She couldn't help but hope that both Leo and Will liked the dress.

"Things got a little out of hand."

"Out of hand?" Leo asked, then reached out and stroked his finger along her shoulder, pressing the hair lying their behind her shoulder.

"Hank." She began to protest him telling his brothers what happened but he interrupted her.

"Credence wants our woman," he said and reached around her waist with his arm, found the zipper to her dress, and began to unzip it.

"I hope you set that fucker straight," Leo said firmly as he ran the back of his knuckles down her other arm, giving her goose bumps and making her nipples harden.

"She's here with us, isn't she?" Hank asked and she gripped her dress against her chest as the material gave out.

She wore no bra. The dress didn't allow for it.

Leo kissed her shoulder on her left side.

"You're going to be our woman, Adel. That means no other men but us," Leo told her as Hank held a firm expression.

"Does that go for the three of you, too? No other women?" she asked, voice cracking.

"Hell yeah, baby. There isn't anyone else we want but you. That's how it's been for quite some time," Leo told her next.

Hank caressed her cheeks and cupped them.

"Say you'll stay with us tonight. Make this official. Become all ours."

He softly kissed her lips and she was overcome with desire. She let go of the material of her dress and let it fall to the floor.

She heard their intake of breath and then felt Hank lift her up and place her on the bed. He knelt with one leg between her thighs as Leo and Will each cupped a breast.

"My God, Adel, you're gorgeous," Leo told her then leaned down and kissed her lips.

She reached up and ran her hand through his hair and soaked up the sparks connecting each of them.

"Are you on birth control or do we need protection?" Hank asked her as he slid her panties from her body then began to kiss her inner calf, her thigh, then all the way to her pussy.

She squirmed and wiggled.

"I have an IUD. I'm safe," she replied, sounding breathless.

Will pulled on her nipple then licked across the tip.

"Will," she exclaimed.

"We are, too," Leo told her and then she felt Hank's mouth and tongue delve into her pussy and she held her breath. She was overwhelmed with this situation. Three men. Three sexy, desirable, older men wanted her. Was this a mistake? Was she ruining herself forever? She thought of her mother, her father, despite her anger toward them both. What would they say or do? How would they react and treat her if they knew she had sex with three men at once?

She felt the tears reach her eyes.

*But I want to. It feels so right. Their touch feels so good.*

"Hank." She grabbed his head and he lifted his mouth from her pussy. The sight of his wet lips, the hunger in his eyes, and his big muscles along his chest and shoulders made her speechless.

He crawled closer, covering her body with his own and cupping her cheeks as he rested on his elbows.

"Talk to me. What's wrong?"

She swallowed hard and then looked to Will and Leo then back to Hank.

"I'm scared," she admitted and felt the tightness in her chest and waited to hear them say she was stupid or acting like a child or being such a prude. That was what Bentley would have told her for saying such a thing.

"Don't be scared. Put aside anything any other man has said or done to you in the past. It doesn't exist. Only me, Leo, and Will do," Hank told her.

A tear escaped her eye as she memorized their expressions, Hank's words, and how perfect it was.

She tilted her head up until her lips touched Hank's. He allowed her this control, this time to prepare to make love to him and his brothers.

She absorbed his taste, his firm lips, and the scent of his cologne as well as the softness of his skin above the protruding muscles.

He kissed her back, and all her fears minimized. She wanted this, and she wanted them.

Hank eased up and his brothers joined in tasting her and feasting on her body. They worked in sync, together, to comfort her, to lessen her fears and bring out such desire and lust she thought she lost her mind.

She reached for Hank's head but Will and Leo were there to hold her arms above her head as they feasted on her breasts.

She watched in awe as Will used his talented tongue to lick, suckle, then twirl around her nipple and areola. Leo did the same on the other side, and tugged and pulled on her nipple, instantly hardening the tiny bud. It was too much as she moaned and shook as her orgasm overtook her body.

"I need in. I need you," Hank told her.

"Yes, yes, Hank, I want you, too."

He aligned his cock with her pussy and pressed the tip to her cunt. She gasped and tightened up and he didn't penetrate. Instead he gripped her hips and her belly, letting his thumbs softly stroke her skin.

"Relax and let me in. I promise I won't hurt you."

She could see the honesty, the care in his eyes as she released a breath and held his gaze.

"Slow, and easy," he whispered and then he began to push the thick, hard muscle deeper and she relaxed and let him in, feeling overwhelmed with emotion.

Leo and Will released her hands and Hank covered her body with his as he lifted her thighs up higher against his hips and began a series of hard, deep strokes. She ran her palms up over his pectoral muscles and admired the ripples of muscles, the dips and ridges of steel beneath her fingertips as he brought out another soft moan from her lips.

"Hank, oh God, you're so big," she told him, feeling every sensation. Her breath got caught in her throat on every stroke of his cock into her pussy. Over and over again he thrust into her until he couldn't go slow anymore.

She held on tight and let him have all of her. There would be no worries about regrets or pain. That was for later. Right now she would relish in their connection and the fact that she was going to make love to Leo and Will next.

* * * *

Hank was shocked at the intensity of emotions he felt as he made love to Adel. With every stroke of his cock he claimed her as his woman, his possession and responsibility. He didn't want this to be temporary. That was a first for him. He didn't do commitments, and he didn't string women along for his own pleasure, but with Adel, he wanted to know she was his forever. That she would stay with him and his brothers and complete their own family. He wanted what his parents had. He wanted to come home to Adel every night and make passionate love to her.

He thrust faster, deeper. His desires and wants and needs were fed by her moans, counterthrusts, and the way her hands gripped his arms as she cried out his name and came again.

"Adel!" he roared as he thrust two more times then shook, leaving his seed in her body and knowing that one day she would carry his child and that of his brothers.

He cupped her cheeks and swept his lips over hers. She kissed him back and they hugged as he rolled to his side, taking her with him and sliding his cock from her pussy.

"So beautiful. God, baby, you're everything." He held her gaze and saw the love, the genuineness in her eyes and he had that twinge of guilt or maybe feeling of inadequacy that told him she was too good for him. For the three of them.

He caressed along her curves, loving her body, the swell of her breasts, her firm, round ass that wasn't small by any means yet not too big. It was in proportion with her body and the thought of exploring it next had him tracing the crack of her ass with his finger.

"Hank," she gasped but she didn't pull away.

Leo joined them, kissing her shoulder.

Hank continued to stroke the crack as he teased her lips with tongue and teeth, tugging on her lower lip.

"Every part of you will belong to us as every part of us will belong to you," he told her and pressed his finger firmer over her hole.

"Roll to your belly, baby. I want to see what has my brother all fired up," Leo said and Hank shifted back as Leo rolled Adel to her belly.

"I think I need a look, too," Will said, joining them at the edge of the bed, spreading Adel's thighs and kissing and licking a pathway to her ass.

"Oh God, this is crazy," she whispered.

Hank ran a hand along her ass cheek as Leo stroked a finger into her cunt.

"Spread wider. Don't tighten up," Will told her and she tilted her pelvis up, giving Leo better access to her pussy.

Hank moved to her back, tracing along her spine as he kissed her shoulder.

"I love your skin. It's soft and sexy," he said and she moaned then lifted higher.

Leo was thrusting his fingers faster into her pussy as Will lifted her hips.

"I need in," he said.

"In a minute. Our woman seems to like getting her pussy fingered as we all watch her ass rock back and forth," Leo said then stroked a little faster.

"Oh God, Leo. Please," she said.

\* \* \* \*

Adel was on fire. She wanted their fingers, their mouths everywhere they were willing to touch. When Leo pulled his fingers from her cunt and then pressed the wet digits against her puckered hole, she nearly shot up off the bed.

Will was there to pull her back against him. Her thighs were wide, her knees on the edge of the bed with Will's thighs holding her open while his thick, long cock tapped against her inner thigh.

Leo continued to stroke the cream from her pussy to her anus, making her body hum for more.

"Please," she begged and then she felt Leo's finger push into her anus. She gasped and tightened up.

*Smack.*

The spank to her ass came from Hank. Cream gushed from her pussy and Leo pulled his finger out and used the cream to lubricate her anus. He pushed the digit right in and she began to rock against it.

Her pussy swelled with need and she gripped the comforter tighter. Leo maneuvered to the side, his forearm resting on her ass cheek as he thrust a little faster. She was rocking and moaning.

*Smack.*

*Smack.*

"Oh God."

"Fuck, Leo, I need in," Will said.

"Then do it."

She felt their bodies adjust slightly then Will's cock began to push into her pussy. It felt thick, hard, and she wondered if he would fit. As Leo stroked her ass, Hank brought his cock to her lips. His expression was firm and she felt so out of control she immediately opened her mouth and took a taste. He smelled like his cologne and her own cream. She licked and suckled his cock as Will pushed deeper until he finally was all the way in. They all began to move. Hank gripped her hair and caressed her cheeks as he pushed his cock in and out of her mouth.

Leo pulled his finger from her ass and began to suckle her breast as Will took over fucking her so hard, so fast she thought she might lose her mind.

*Smack, smack, smack.*

His consecutive smacks to her ass with his thrusts sent her over the edge and Hank, too.

Hank grunted and came, shooting his seed down her throat. She cried out after she swallowed him then released his cock as Will gripped her hips and plunged so hard the bed shook and creaked. She gripped the comforter and then Will came calling her name.

Just as she tried to recover, Will pulled out and Leo gripped her hips, lifted her up and over him, aligning his cock with her pussy, and pulled her hips down as he thrust his hips upward.

She grabbed his shoulders and cried out again.

It was too much. They were so big and hard, she lost her breath.

"Oh God."

She locked gazes with Leo and his dark brown eyes.

"I love the way your tits sway with every thrust. Fuck, baby, you're hot. So fucking hot and all ours."

His fingers dug into her hips as he thrust hard upward then rolled her to her back. She gasped and held onto him then kissed him deeply while he pounded into her body, sending her deeper into the mattress and comforters.

She ran her fingers through his hair and cheered him on.

"Yes, Leo. More, Leo. Please harder, harder," she said as her body tightened and the sensations intensified.

"Adel. Holy fuck," he said and lifted her thighs up over his shoulders, sending her to balance on her shoulder blades as he fucked her with all he had.

His large hands were everywhere and he gripped her as she cried out his name, coming hard. He followed suit and shook and shivered against her.

"Sweet mother that was fucking great," he said as he lowered her legs, cupped her cheeks, and kissed her hard on the mouth. He rolled her to her side and squeezed her to him, his cock still in her cunt even though it softened.

"Right here is where you belong always. With me and my brothers," Leo said and kissed her. Will joined them on the bed, kissing her shoulder and caressing her hip as Hank caressed her calves and ankles.

"You're staying the night, Adel," Hank told her.

"I don't know if that's such a good idea," she said.

"You're staying, and get used to it." He ran his hand up her thigh to her ass, giving it a squeeze. All three brothers were touching her.

"You belong to the Ferguson men now. There's no turning back." He gave her ass a smack and she was overwhelmed with emotions. This was real. This was going to work out. Everything would be fine with Will, Hank, and Leo in her corner. Always.

# Chapter 5

Adel felt the fingers tracing along her spine and then another set of hands caressing her thighs wider. She was on her belly and hugging an arm.

As she blinked her eyes open she saw Hank staring at her and caressing her shoulder. It was his arm she was hugging.

"Good morning, gorgeous," he whispered.

She felt her legs part wider and then a finger pressed up into her pussy.

She moaned as she tilted her head back and saw Will.

"Did you sleep well?" Leo asked her and kissed her other shoulder. She nodded her head.

Hank caressed the hair from her cheek. "You talk in your sleep. Did you know that?" he asked.

"No, I didn't." She released his arm and lifted up, giving Will better access to her cunt and also giving her more room to explore Hank's body.

She leaned over and kissed his chest then rolled her tongue over his nipple as she lifted her thigh higher.

She moaned softly as Will's fingers thrust deeper.

"That feels good," Hank told her and gripped her wrist gently as she ran her palm along his pectoral muscles.

"What did I say in my sleep?" she asked Hank.

"That you need us and want us everywhere," Leo told her then leaned down and kissed her shoulder as he trailed a finger along her ass cheek.

"Really? Anything else?" she asked.

"That you want my cock in your ass while Hank fucks your pussy and you suck Will's cock," Leo said and knelt up.

She lifted up, leaning on her hands as she looked at Leo.

He was so serious and as her heart fluttered and her belly did a series of twists and turns she knew she wanted that, too.

"I said that in my sleep huh?" she challenged him.

"You were begging for it," Hank told her and then cupped her cheeks and plunged his tongue into her mouth.

She felt Will's fingers leave her pussy and Hank pulled her onto his lap. He maneuvered her to his liking and then she felt his hand move between them. She knew what he wanted. Hell, she knew what she wanted. All three of them inside of her completing this little group.

She lifted up and took Hank's cock up into her pussy. He scooted lower on the bed and gripped her hips as she began to ride him.

Will knelt closer, his cock in his hand and a smile on his face. He reached out with his free hand and cupped her breasts. He ran his thumb over the nipple and then tugged.

"I love these breasts. I can feast on them for hours." He leaned forward and kissed her breast then suckled on the tip. She felt his cock tap against her side and then she felt Leo behind her licking along the crack of her ass.

She gasped.

"I need that mouth, baby. We're going to be one. We're going to make love together," Will said and she licked her lips, swallowed the feelings of trepidation, and opened wide for Will's cock.

Just as she slid her tongue along the shaft then cupped his balls in her hand, she felt the cool liquid against her ass.

"Just getting it nice and lubricated for my cock. Don't want to hurt our woman," Leo told her then kissed her shoulder.

Hank began to thrust upward slowly as she tried focusing on sucking Will's cock, but the feeling of Leo's fingers thrusting and spreading her anus was making her lose her train of thought. She started rocking back against his fingers and all hell broke loose.

Hank was thrusting upward faster, and Will was gripping her hair and stroking into her mouth. Then she felt Leo pull his fingers from her ass and then she felt the tip of his cock. Slowly, as not to hurt her, Leo began to push slowly into her ass. Back and forth he worked the thick, hard muscle into her anus. She tried to relax, her feelings overwhelmed her and then Hank spoke to her.

"Let him in. Let us love you together, because together is what we'll be for a very long time."

"That's it, baby, relax those inner muscles and let us claim you our woman," Leo said and inched a little deeper.

He was big. Maybe too big as he pulled a little out then slowly pushed back in.

She closed her eyes and relished the combined sensations. She wanted to please them, to let go with them and be part of them always.

She felt Leo push deeper until she felt the *plop* sensation and he was all the way in.

Leo held himself deep then eased out. He stroked back and forth sending her nerve endings on full alert. Meanwhile Hank slowed his pace and they counterthrusted. She was never without a cock inside her. Even as Leo pulled out, Hank thrust forward and so did Will, but Will's cock was growing thicker and she knew he would come.

She pinched his balls and that was it. He thrust into her mouth and he came. She licked him clean and then held on for the ride as Hank and Leo worked their cocks into her body over and over again.

She was strung so tight she thought she might scream her head off as both men thrust faster and harder. She knew the moment when she broke and there was no more reason to hold back. She let go and screamed her release. Hank and Leo followed then held her in their arms and kissed her until exhaustion overtook her once more.

* * * *

"So you didn't exactly explain what happened last night at the fundraising dinner? You were pretty damn fired up," Leo said to Hank as they worked in the kitchen preparing breakfast. Will and Adel were upstairs. Adel was taking a shower.

"One minute she and I are talking to Michelle Morrison and Credence and the next I'm being dragged across the room to the bidding table and surrounded by some female vultures looking to flirt. I glance across the room to check on Adel, who immediately caught Credence's attention, the slimy bastard, and JT and JR join them. Credence had his hand on her lower back as if he owned her. The fuck," Hank said and ran his fingers through his hair. Hearing that, especially after what they all shared last night, Leo was pissed, too.

"I would have knocked that dick out for touching our woman. Didn't you let on that it was a date and you were involved with Adel?"

"Not exactly. She was talking a mile a minute with the Morrison brothers and Credence. Got them talking about the project and she was giving them some info on our proposal. When I joined them what really set me off was how Credence was offering to help her personally with any questions she might have about the bidding project and proposal. You know what he fucking meant by personal," Hank told Leo.

"I'll rip his fucking head off if I even see him flirt with Adel, never mind touch her. She won't have further contact with him."

"Leo?"

Leo turned around to hear Adel's voice. She was standing in the doorway wearing her dress from last night and holding her heels by the straps.

He licked his lower lip and held her gaze.

"If Credence calls you out of the blue, or tries to ask you out or to meet him, you better damn well let me know." He raised his voice.

Adel took a retreating step back and Leo widened his eyes. He was being a jerk.

"Ah shit, Adel." He stalked toward her and pulled her into his arms hugging her.

"I'm sorry. Hank got me all riled up and well, I was fucking jealous."

He pulled back and looked down into her eyes. She was so petite and sexy, plus she smelled like their soap and shampoo.

"Before last night I felt protective of you. I always have felt that way, but after what we shared last night and what I hope will come of this relationship, I feel possessive. I can't apologize for that, but I can try not to be so abrupt."

"Or sound so untrusting?" she asked, raising one of her eyebrows up at him.

He chuckled and caressed her cheek. "Or untrusting." He lowered his mouth to hers and kissed her and he was relieved when she hugged him in return.

"I can't make the same promise," Hank stated as he brought the eggs and bacon over toward the table.

Adel looked at him as Leo guided her back toward the table.

"What's mine is mine. Someone tries to take you from me or move in on what's mine and forget it. You don't want to know," he said firmly.

Leo watched Adel hold Hank's gaze.

Hank lifted his finger and curled it back and forth toward him for Adel to come to him. She hesitated only a moment and then walked the few feet to meet Hank.

Hank stared down into her eyes.

"Last night was incredible. No regrets, only promises of even better nights together. You're ours now, Adel. Part of us. Do you understand?"

She nodded her head. Hank smiled softly.

He reached over her shoulder, under her hair to cup her head, and then kissed her, pulling her up against his chest. Adel kissed him back until Will entered the kitchen.

"Are we having food for breakfast or Adel?"

Leo chuckled as he Hank released Adel.

"I think I like the sound of having Adel for breakfast," Leo said and chuckled as he saw her cheeks turn a nice shade of pink.

Will walked closer, and he looked at the table of food then at Adel.

"Or maybe we can strip her naked, lay her on the table, then eat our breakfast right off of her body. Maybe drizzle a little syrup along her nipples, then down her belly and over her pussy," Will said as he trailed his finger along her body.

Hank ran his hand under her dress then to her pussy.

"No syrup necessary, her pussy is sweet and delicious enough."

She smacked his hand away and turned around to sit down.

"I think we should sit down now," she said and Leo, Hank, and Will chuckled. Leo looked at his brothers. He hadn't seen them smile like this and act so happy in a long time. Leo squeezed Adel's shoulders. It was all because of her. Adel was meant to be theirs and nothing would stand in their way of happiness.

# **Chapter 6**

"You haven't returned any of our calls. It's been three weeks."

"I've been busy with work and things, Mom. Besides, I wouldn't return any of Bentley's calls anyway. There's no need for me to."

Adel was standing in her bedroom trying to get ready for work. The men and her submitted the proposal to Credence and the team at Morrison's company. If all went well they would be celebrating with their fathers and mom at dinner on Friday evening. She had yet to hear from Credence with any feedback but perhaps today.

She straightened out the navy blue dress she wore and stepped into the low-heeled pumps. Hank loved the color blue on her. She smiled and then heard her mom's voice cut into her thoughts.

"Are you even listening to me? What is wrong with you? What aren't you telling me?"

So badly she wanted to tell her mom about Hank, Will, and Leo and how much in love she was with them. Her mom was on her father's side and despite claiming to want Adel to be happy, Adel didn't think her mom really did want that. She allowed her husband to control her, manipulate her, and do whatever he told her to. That wasn't the life Adel wanted.

"I have a lot going on, Mom. Work is crazy busy and then I try to hang out with friends."

"Friends or are you seeing someone?" Her mom's question surprised her.

"Oh God, Adel, what if Bentley finds out? He won't be happy. He wants you back."

"Well I don't want him back. I don't need a man like that in my life. One that can hurt me, abuse me, and cheat on me. No thank you. We've been over this before."

"So does this mean you won't ever come back here to visit me, or to see your father? He's not feeling well."

"You've been saying that for a month. Is he really ill, or does he just want to see me and tell me how wrong I was to leave Bentley?"

"You're his daughter. He wants what's best for you."

"No, Mom, he wants what's best for him and for making money."

"Bentley bought out your father's shares. He no longer is part of the business. He wanted to wipe his hands clean of what he had done, selling you out for that company merge."

Adel was shocked. Could her dad really have done that to make up for what he had done over a year ago? It was in that moment that she felt a bit of hope or need to have the love of her father as his only baby girl. Then she felt that twist of uncertainty. She could move on freely and without such fears and reservations with Hank, Leo, and Will, giving them her full trust, if she could forgive her father and just move on. She realized that if she saw him and even if he were only slightly remorseful that it would be enough to forgive him.

"Adel, please consider coming home for a visit. Whatever you have going on, put on hold to see your father. You mean so much to him. Not having you here has shown him that."

Adel felt the tears reach her eyes.

"I'll think about it. I need to go right now. I'm going to be late for work."

"Promise me you'll come home for a visit."

She was hesitant but the tone of her mom's voice, the sincerity, the sadness made her want to please her even after all this time and what her own family had done to her.

"I'll call you later in the week to confirm when." She disconnected the call then stared at herself in the mirror.

"I can do this. I can forgive Dad, see them in person, and let them see how well I am without Bentley in my life and I can move on with Hank, Leo, and Will."

\* \* \* \*

"You're out of your mind. Why would you expose yourself to their negativity and lies? What if it's a plan to hurt you or put you down and minimize what you've accomplished? What if they find out about Hank, Leo, and Will?" Marlena asked Adel.

"She's right. From what you've told us, your parents aren't exactly the loving supportive types," Alicia added.

"I know," Adel replied as she lowered her eyes and held the coffee cup between her hands. Then she felt Mercedes's hand cover hers.

"Then why expose yourself to their negativity? Hank, Will, Leo, and all of us are your family now. We support you, love you, and believe in you."

Adel smiled softly.

"I love all of you, too. It's just that I think I need to do this. To move on with Hank, Will, and Leo and truly give them all of me, including my heart and my trust. I'm still holding back."

"So you think if you forgive your father then those insecurities will disappear?" Marlena asked her and Adel nodded her head.

"I'm not sure that's going to work, and what if you go there and they aren't so kind and you can't forgive them, then what?" Mercedes asked.

"At least I know that I tried. That I did everything in my power to make it work and to move on and have some kind of relationship with my father."

"You're a kind person, Adel, but I hope that you realize if this doesn't work out and your parents try to put you down and disapprove of what your life is like without them, that you'll know you don't need them and that you have us," Alicia said to her.

"It's a risk. I know."

"Are you going to tell them about Hank, Leo, and Will?" Mercedes asked.

"Better yet, are you going to tell Hank, Will, and Leo about what your father did, and about Bentley and this idea of forgiving your father?" Alicia asked.

Adel shook her head.

"I'll tell them when I return. Otherwise, knowing how protective they are, they'll want to go with me. I need to do this solo."

Mercedes wasn't certain that this was the right decision for Adel to make, but who was she to stand in her way and try to give an opinion? She didn't have half the self-confidence that Adel and the others had. Mercedes was scared. She knew what it was like to be on her own, to fend for herself, and to not even get three meals a day. For a year she lived on eating once a day. Life had thrown her many curveballs and she often wished for the things other people had. She would love to have a family, relatives, someone who she could love and who could love her, but that just wasn't the case. She looked at Adel, who had a family, and that family hurt her, sold her out, and left her with nothing but heartache. Yet still Adel wanted to forgive them so she could move on.

Mercedes's life was so different. She'd had two disabled, sickly parents who she cared for and helped keep comfortable until they died. She couldn't work, couldn't go to college until much later and now here she was twenty-six years old and she was tired and felt hollow inside, but at least she had these three women as her friends. She cherished the friendship that continued to grow. She longed to have love, to find love the way the three women found it, but she wasn't hopeful. She just didn't think she had any more in her heart to give after all she gave and sacrificed for her parents. Living on the streets, surviving on her own, hardened her heart in many ways.

Maybe she could learn from someone like Adel and her ability to forgive and forget. Maybe.

* * * *

The week had passed and there wasn't any return feedback about the business proposal. As Adel set some papers onto Leo's desk in his office she heard the door close and then the lock click. Turning around she gripped the desk as she laid eyes on Leo. His gaze was intense, his eyes roamed over her body, and in a flash he was right in front of her, pulling her into his arms and kissing her deeply.

She felt it, too. That intense need to have one of her men inside of her. She felt obsessed and tried to hide her feelings from them. She didn't want the men to think she was some psycho woman who would latch on and need them constantly. That would be clingy, annoying, and totally not normal.

She felt Leo lift the hem of her dress and his fingers curled under the material of her panties, finding her pussy before he plunged his fingers deeply into her. She gasped, pulling her mouth from his as she held onto his shoulders.

"I need you. Walking around in this sexy purple dress and watching the material flap against your thighs as you walk past my office was torture." He nipped her neck and licked a pathway down to her breasts. His fingers pumped harder, deeper, faster.

She gripped his shoulders as he spread her legs when her ass landed on his hard desk.

"Leo, please, we can't do this here. It's unprofessional."

He pulled from her neck and stared into her eyes.

"Unprofessional? You want to know what's unprofessional? The fact that all I can think about is listening to your sweet, kind voice as you talk on the phone, watch you and that sincere, intense expression on your face as you type on your computer, and know that I can't sink my cock balls deep into your pussy or in your ass because I'm at work and trying to be professional. Fuck professional." He unzipped his pants and she felt his erection. His words, his intensity had her pushing down her own panties as he lowered his pants and lifted her hips then thrust his hard, thick cock into her pussy. She held onto his shoulders as he rocked back and forth and gripped her ass and hips so tight she knew he would leave marks but she didn't care. She thrust back and clenched her teeth to stop herself from screaming his name.

The desk didn't make a sound. The heavy, thick oak handled Leo's thrusts.

She felt her body tighten. This was so naughty, so risky and knowing that employees were right outside the door and down the hallway and that his brother Hank was probably wondering why she hadn't come back to take notes in his office, all aroused her as she came hard, shaking and gasping for breath.

"I love you. I hope that doesn't scare you. I love you," he said as he came inside of her, shocking her speechless.

He kissed her deeply then reached to the side for tissues.

He chuckled.

"It's all I have," he said as he slowly pulled from her body.

His cock slid out and she felt the loss. She had it so bad. In fact, as she cleaned herself up with his assistance and they fixed their clothes, she thought about visiting Will and Hank next. It came natural. She couldn't have one of them and not the other two as well.

She chuckled and felt Leo's hands slide along her dress over her ass and fix the material.

"What were you just thinking about?" he asked as he fixed his dress shirt and she helped him with his pants.

"Visiting Will and Hank's office next," she said.

His eyes darkened and a sinful smile formed on his lips.

"So glad you said that. Hank is expecting you. Then Will." He turned her around, gave her ass a spank, and on trembling legs she headed out of the office.

There wasn't a soul in sight. It was too good to be true. With her luck someone would come by looking for her then knock on Hank's door.

She took a sip of her water bottle and felt her nipples harden. The buzzer on her desk went off and she jumped.

"Adel, in my office now," Hank told her.

"Yes, sir," she replied all efficientlike. She glanced around. Still no one was in sight.

She headed to his door, knocked, and entered.

There Hank stood in front of his desk, arms crossed, a determined angry expression on his face and she paused.

"Yes, sir, you needed me?" she asked, the words doing a number to her cunt and her legs.

"Close the door." She reached back and closed it.

"Where were you? I asked you to come in here fifteen minutes ago."

"Leo needed me."

She couldn't believe how turned on she was right now.

"Well I need you, too. Come here," he said and as she approached he stood his ground and didn't move. He didn't uncross his arms as he took in the sight of her.

"Closer," he told her, making her shiver with desire as she stepped right up to him.

He looked her over.

"You look a little flushed. What exactly did Leo need you for?" he asked.

She lowered her eyes.

"Look at me." She snapped her head back up, surprised by his tone and authority but also turned on by it.

"What did he need from you?"

She was so aroused. She was shocked by the words that came into her head.

"I expect the truth. Remember when I said to you if I ask you a question then I want an answer?"

"Yes, sir."

His eyes widened and he uncrossed his arms but instead of putting his hands on her like she hoped, he gripped the desk.

"What did he want from you? The truth."

"My body," she whispered and he clenched his teeth. She could see his cheek cave in a little.

He looked her over again.

"Which part of your body?"

*Oh brother.*

She took an uneasy breath and then wondered if she could say the words.

"Are you hiding something from me? Do you need that ass spanked?"

She panicked, knowing that a spanking from Hank would send her over the edge. Her pussy leaked and she tightened her thighs together.

"He wanted my pussy."

Hank gave a small smirk.

"That's interesting, because that's what I want from you, too."

He snagged an arm around her waist, pulled her close, and kissed her. In a flash his hands were lifting the bottom of her dress and shoving them to her waist. He pressed her panties down and cool air collided with her pussy. She moaned into his mouth as she cupped his balls against his dress pants and he released her lips. "Feeling a bit frisky huh?" he asked and then nipped her neck.

She moaned and then he pulled back, turned her around, and pressed her body over the desk.

"I thought about fucking you over this desk for months. That you would come in here with your sweet voice calling me sir, serving me coffee, and then serving me this sweet, wet cunt." He thrust fingers into her pussy from behind as she gripped the desk. Something came over her as she lifted up and shoved back.

"I thought about that, too. You ordering me to lay here while you had your way with me."

"Sounds like we all had the same idea."

Adel was shocked to hear Will's voice, but Hank didn't seem shocked at all as he undid his pants, pushed them down, and spread her thighs.

"Someone didn't lock the door behind them," Will stated and she felt her cheeks turn red. Anyone could have come into the room and caught them like this. Will locked gazes with her.

"That's going to cost you some serious punishment."

She lifted up but Hank pressed his cock to her pussy. "You can give her that punishment as soon as I'm done. Seems she's had some naughty thoughts, too, and didn't share them."

Hank lifted her hips and slid his cock into her pussy.

Adel gasped and Hank didn't slow down. He began a series of fast, deep thrusts into her pussy from behind as he held her hips.

"Fuck her pussy real good, bro. She's in a lot of trouble," Will said and she saw him pull something from his pocket then undo his shirt. The thought that he would have sex with her next had her panting and creaming. The sound of Hank's balls slapping against her ass as she moaned and counterthrusted filled the room.

"She's a really naughty girl, Will. Was just fucking Leo in his office only a few minutes ago."

"So I heard. Don't worry. I know exactly how to punish her," Will said and she saw the tube of lube as he slapped it against his hand.

"Fuck she feels so good. Damn, baby, I really did fantasize about this, about having you any fucking time I want you. Fuck," Hank said and slapped her ass as he thrust faster.

The sight of the lube, knowing that Will would take her ass after, made her come. She moaned and slapped her hand over her mouth as she came.

"Fuck," Hank cursed as he shot his load and then leaned over her, moving her hair off her neck and kissing her.

But as she caught her breath and tried to recover, Hank pulled out and there was Will taking his place. Cool liquid collided with her anus and slick fingers pushed into her ass. Her entire body hummed and zinged with need. Tiny vibrations erupted through her and she moaned and pressed back. Instantly her pussy swelled and felt full and needy.

*Smack.*

*Smack.*

*Smack.*

Will slapped her ass as he thrust slick fingers into her lubricated ass. Over and over again he smacked her ass then spread her thighs with his thighs. She felt the material of his shirt brush against the skin on her back, tickling her and arousing her. She moaned again and then felt the thick, hard cock push against the tight bud.

"Oh fuck, she looks incredible," Hank said.

"She feels incredible. I love fucking this ass, owning this ass, making her all mine," Will said.

*Smack.*

He smacked her ass then pushed his cock through the tight rings until he could go no further.

"Oh God, Will. Oh God."

"Shhh, baby. We don't want to give away exactly what we're doing in here now do we?" Hank asked her as he caressed her hair from her face.

"Fuck she's so tight. Damn, baby, you're wild. You make us so happy," Will told her.

She felt her heart soar and she knew they made her happy, too. Her pussy was on fire and she needed desperately to come and be touched there. Will reached under and touched her pussy with his fingers.

"Yes, oh God, Will, please I need more," she told him and he stroked her cunt, running the cream over her pussy lips back and forth, but it wasn't enough.

She shoved his hands to the side as she reached under her as Will lifted her hips and stroked into her ass and she fingered herself.

"Holy fucking shit," Will said.

"What?" Hank asked.

"She's fingering herself. Holy fuck I'm gonna come. Come with me, Adel. Finger that pussy good, let go and come with me," he ordered.

She felt her body tighten as she fingered her cunt and thrust back against Will's cock. Her ass burned, her pussy swelled, and she saw the black spots in front of her eyes as cream poured from her pussy and she came. Will grunted and held her tight against him as he came just as hard. They lay there for a few moments and she couldn't move. She was sated, well loved, and couldn't even think about returning to her desk.

As Will eased his cock from her ass, he turned her around and kissed her deeply. She hugged him tight.

"Life in the office will never be the same again. I love you, baby. You're perfect and all ours," he told her and she hugged him back wishing she could say she loved him, too, but knowing she needed to take care of her father first.

\* \* \* \*

Adel was sitting in the meeting room with Leo, Will, and Hank going over some blueprints on another job and she was taking notes. Hank watched her and smiled as Will placed his hand on her knee for the dozenth time and she pushed it off, reminding him about being professional. He of course teased her relentlessly.

They heard the knock on the door and their fathers Harold and William entered. They greeted them hello and of course gave Adel kisses and hugs hello before they sat down.

"So we heard that another company has bid on the job with Morrisons and their price is twenty thousand dollars under your bid," William said.

"Twenty thousand?" Leo asked and they nodded.

"What company?" Hank asked.

"I don't know. They're not supposed to say but I put in a call to Michelle Morrison. She was very impressed with Adel a few weeks ago at the fundraising event and so were her sons. Surprisingly even Credence complimented her which Michelle was shocked at," Harold told them.

Hank gave her a look and she gave a soft smile in return. He didn't like thinking about other men liking her and wanting her. He was possessive.

"I wonder who it could be. Maybe Delphi construction out of Charlotte? They're pretty big?" Will asked and they all threw out a few names and then Harold's phone rang.

"It's Michelle," he whispered and then stood up and answered the phone. Hank listened to his dad make small talk and then he got quiet and said thank you and then listened before he hung up the phone.

"Well?" Will asked.

Harold glanced at Adel and then looked at his sons.

Hank wondered why he did that.

"Ross McK Construction."

Adel gasped and then she quickly looked at Harold.

"Well they're not as great as us. They are new to the business in the last five years when two companies merged, but I hear they have been having financial problems. They're probably hoping to land this job to gain some momentum to keep in business. I'm certain the Morrisons will give us the opportunity to come back and counter if necessary," Harold said.

"Counter? At twenty-thousand less? I don't think so. We came as close as we could. Those guys are cutthroating us. Who the hell are they?" Leo asked as he stood up.

Hank watched Adel as she stood up next.

"I can call Credence and see if there's room to counter or if they are leaning toward this company or yours?" Adel suggested.

"No, I don't want you talking to him," Hank said and stood up.

"Hank, this is business and you're being silly. I can handle Credence. He knows I'm involved with you and your brothers," she said as she took her papers and book and headed toward the door.

"I'll walk you out," Harold said. She nodded her head and left the room. Hank listened to his brothers and their father go over other ideas and try to figure out who Ross McK Construction was. He didn't know why, but he had a bad feeling in his gut. Something wasn't right.

* * * *

"Adel, I'm sorry. If I had gotten that call ten minutes earlier I would have saved you from hearing it that way," Harold told her. Adel shook her head.

"Do you think he's doing this to get back at me? I mean I know he can find out where I live and work, but would he take it this far?"

"Of course he would. Even though the deal was with your dad and over marrying you and merging companies the man still had it bad for you. You took his control and power away from him when you left him."

She looked toward the office door.

"I'm supposed to leave tomorrow to see my parents."

"What? No, why?" he asked.

"Because my mom said my dad wants to make amends and to be honest with you, I can't even tell your sons I love them and I can't give them all of me until I forgive my dad, put the past behind me, and move on. I'm going to give it a try. If he hasn't changed then at least I tried."

"And what about Bentley and this whole business with submitting a proposal?"

"I suppose I'll have to handle that with my dad when I see him. My mom said that Bentley pushed him out of the business and bought out his stocks in the company, but my dad isn't stupid. I'm not saying that I matter that much, obviously, but if he was going to give up his daughter and sell out for money and a business deal, that deal was going to be successful."

"I don't like this idea of you going there alone. Have you told my sons anything?"

She shook her head. "If I tell them about Bentley they'll flip and won't let me go. If I tell them about the company they'll feel badly for me and then look at me as weak and feel sorry for me, but if I go talk to my parents, cut the ties, find closure, and maybe even figure out their interest in this construction job, then I can come back here and explain everything to the guys."

"Will you tell your parents about the relationship with my sons?" Harold asked.

"I don't know. I guess it depends on whether or not their request for me to come visit is honestly about forgiveness or just about control and how they think they still have power over me. I don't know, but I have to end this. I have to put the past behind me in order to move on with Hank, Will, and Leo. I have to."

\* \* \* \*

"Are you certain that she's sleeping with all three of them?" Bentley asked the snitch he had working in Ferguson construction and keeping an eye on his girl.

"Yes, sir, she's involved with all three of them. If you ask me, they moved in quickly and seduced her. They have quite the reputations. A lot of other guys are pretty pissed off."

"She's a beautiful woman, but I wasn't expecting this. I'll deal with it soon enough. Besides, I've got the information and the pictures you gathered for me on the three men. Looks like they enjoy screwing around with women."

"Well those are from a year ago. To be honest, the three men haven't shown an interest in other women for the better part of a year. I only came here on your request and a month after Adel was hired."

"Doesn't matter. She'll see these pictures and I'll tell her they're more recent. She'll see the men making out, practically having sex against the cars with different women. That should piss off Adel and force her closer to me. I've got a plan. You stick to yours and keep me posted on any changes or updates."

Bentley disconnected the call and looked into the mirror. He straightened out his bow tie on his tux. Adel hadn't a clue that he was going to be at the small dinner party at her parent's house tonight. He couldn't wait. If all went as planned, she would be sleeping in his bed tonight whether she was ready for that or not.

He walked across the room and grabbed the small envelope of pictures. He tucked them into the inside pocket of his jacket and headed out the door. Tonight he'd get his woman back and ensure that she never returned to Chance again.

\* \* \* \*

"Mom, this dress is gorgeous but I wish you would have told me about the dinner party. I thought Dad wanted to talk."

"He does want to talk but you know when he gets a business deal going that it can interfere in personal lives. Just mingle a little, more guests are arriving and then dinner will be served," her mom told her.

Adel watched Gladys McKinley socializing and making sure that everyone was enjoying themselves. Adel hated these events. Everyone was decked out in designer gowns and tuxedoes and turning their noses up to others around them and even to people they just smiled at and talked cordially to. They were all fake, and she was starting to think that she should just leave. It would be an hour drive but it was better than staying here. She missed Hank, Leo, and Will. She just wanted to head back to Chance to be with them instead of standing here waiting to see her father and to hear what he had to say.

"Adel, your father wants you to meet him in his study downstairs," her mom told her as she passed by and headed toward another group of people. Her mom flew from group to group trying to impress these phonies. She wished she hadn't come here.

She made her way down the hallway and toward the complete other end of the house. If her dad was having a dinner party why would he be so far away from his guests? She stopped trying to figure him out years ago.

She got to the hallway his office was in and knocked on the door.

She entered and no one was in there. She hesitated to leave, that old feeling of getting in trouble for not obeying an order jumped into her head. How silly was she?

"Good evening, Adel."

Her heart pounded inside of her chest at the sound of Bentley's voice.

She turned to look up at him. She took a retreating step back. He looked her over with hunger in his eyes and stepped closer. He kissed her cheek and she stepped away only for him to snag her around the waist and pull her back.

"Don't run from me, Adel. There's so much for us to talk about."

"No, there isn't. I'm not here to see you. I'm here to see my father."

He stepped back but not too far. She was within a small reach of him.

"That's right. Rick mentioned his concerns over your current lifestyle and choice of employment." She immediately was on the defensive.

"That's right. Your constructing company is trying to land the same job as Ferguson construction. Why is that?"

He eyed her over, and the door opened again. This time her dad was there.

"Adel," he said to her. No hug, no sympathetic smile or show of apology. This was some sort of setup. She was mad and she immediately got on the defensive.

"What's this all about? Why are you trying to land a job my friends' construction company is bidding on?" she asked.

"Your friends? Interesting, I've heard otherwise," Bentley said and she cringed. If her father found out about Hank, Will, and Leo and her sexual involvement with them, this conversation could get ugly.

"What is it you want? Did you bring me here under false pretenses? Mom said you wanted to apologize," she said to her father.

"Apologize? I think it's you who should be apologizing to me. You took off when we had an agreement," her father stated.

She was shocked and felt the tears reach her eyes. She had been so stupid. Mercedes, even Harold, were right, her father and Bentley couldn't be trusted and would only hurt her more.

"I'm not doing this." She turned to leave but Bentley grabbed her arm and pulled her back. He gave her a shove toward her father's desk.

"Your daughter needs discipline as I told you years ago."

"She made a mistake, but she's back here now," her father said.

"I'm not back here. I came to visit because Mom said you wanted to make amends."

"I wanted to bring you back to reality. Working in some shitty little family-owned construction company as a secretary fetching coffee is below us."

"I do more than fetch coffee," she replied.

"So I've heard. Perhaps your father would be interested to know about your three bosses and their interest in you."

Her father's eyes widened.

"Harold's and William's sons?" Bentley didn't need to be specific. It seemed her father figured it out right away. His face turned red.

"You should have stayed here with Bentley. Knowing what he knows about your indiscretions, I'm surprised he wants you back." Her father headed toward the door.

She was angry as she looked toward him and raised her voice.

"I'm in love with them and they love me. That's something you know nothing about."

He turned to look at her with disgust and hatred in his eyes. Her own father, the man she thought still could love her.

"You're nothing but a whore. I'm done with you. Bentley, do as you please, the deal is still good. Take her."

Her father slammed the door closed behind him and Adel reached for the handle to chase after him and tell him how evil and mean he really was. Bentley grabbed her arm and turned her around.

"You're wrong you know. They don't love you. They're using you like they used the others."

"You're a liar, Bentley. You're wrong and I'm going back."

She went to turn to leave and he shoved her against the door.

"I'm not lying. They fuck women whenever they want. Against cars, in their offices, anywhere they please." He reached into his pocket as she tried to push him away.

"Look at these. Look for yourself and see."

She caught sight of the images. Will with his hands under a woman's dress, her one leg lifted up against his leg as he pressed her against his sports car.

She took the pictures from his hands and walked toward the front of her father's desk.

She went through the photographs, her heart sinking with every picture and the sight of the three men she loved screwing different women in different places.

"Where did you get these?"

"I have my ways, Adel. I told you that I love you and wanted you in my life under my protection where you belong. I know where you live, and the small cottage you own. I know everything about Ferguson's company and how much you help them. They're using you, and when they've had their fill, their fun, they'll leave you used and jobless. Didn't you know about the many personal assistants they have gone through?"

"They didn't work out. The three of them are too demanding and a lot of secretaries friend them intimidating."

He shook his head. "No, sweetie. They fucked them all and then fired them."

She felt the tears reach her eyes. Could that be true? Was he lying? She felt the tears fill her eyes and her vision blurred.

"If this is the lesson you needed to learn in order to come back to me then so be it. They're not who they said they were. My company is going to land that job and not them because of what they did to you."

"No, no, this is a lie. You're making it up. I don't believe you."

She stared to head toward the door when he lashed out. He struck her across the cheekbone and she cried out.

He grabbed her by her arm and pressed her against the desk.

"You're not going back to them. You're going to stay here with me and be my wife, my lover, and we're going to own this company together."

"Let go of me," she said, her voice shaking.

"You're coming home with me tonight. You're never going back there. It's over and once I fuck you in every hole you'll never think of those dicks again," he said as he cupped her pussy.

Adel slapped him across the face so hard she left a hand mark. She was so shocked that her own reaction and the fact that she fought back, that she didn't put her hands up to defend herself. Bentley swung hard, striking her. He punched her in the ribs, smacked her across the mouth, splitting her lips, and she screamed for him to stop. He slammed her back against the desk and she cried out, the pain so bad she could hardly breathe. He ripped her dress and grabbed at her thighs as he tried undoing his pants with his other hand. She swung at him and begged him to stop but he wouldn't. She was so scared, she was shaking, and her back was in pain from him slamming her down on it. She reached around the desk as he scratched her thighs and ripped her panties. She was screaming and crying when she grabbed the marble pen holder, gripped it tight, and swung it at his face. He was stunned from the hit as she tried getting up to get away from him. He grabbed at her, ripping her top, scratching her breast, and she swung the marble holder again this time hitting him in the temple.

Bentley was stunned and she ran for the door, pulled it open, and ran down the hallway for help. Before she could reach the party her mother was standing there shocked as she covered her mouth and then told her to come with her.

She didn't know if she should believe her or not but the pain in her back and the other injuries were kicking in. Her mom led her down the hall and to another room.

"Call the police. He tried to rape me," Adel said as she cried.

"No police, Adel. No one can know about this." She tried standing up but her mom held her hand.

"Adel, you have to trust me. No one will believe you. Bentley has connections. He'll destroy your life, your reputation, and you'll have nothing."

She shook her head.

"You're wrong. Maybe you've been too weak to fight but not me," she said to her mother as her eyes swelled and her lip burned. She felt like she got hit by a truck and didn't want to walk but knew she had to get out of there.

"Listen to me. I know you believe you can't trust me because of how I got you here, but what I say is true. If you try to press charges they'll backfire on you. He'll use the fact that you're intimate with three men. He'll claim you're a whore and that someone else beat you up and that you're after his money. He owns lawyers and politicians, and he'll destroy your life. Just run away and never come back here."

Adel was crying. She felt so hollow inside and in this moment she realized how weak, how disappointing her own mother was. She didn't fight for herself so why would she fight for Adel?

Adel tried to stand up, the pain in her back immense. She was a mess. Her mom helped her.

"I'll get you out the side so he can't find you."

Her mom had to help her up. They headed down the side hallway and out the door. Adel couldn't believe this was happening to her, but she couldn't give up and she couldn't let Bentley rape her and make her belong to him, too.

She got into her car and by the grace of God she drove all the way to her cottage. She cried until there were no more tears left and when she made it home she realized that she couldn't get out of the car. The adrenaline rush was over, the pain even worse, and the swelling intense. She didn't know who to call or if she should. She couldn't let her men see her this way, and she couldn't call Harold or he would tell his sons.

She grabbed her cell phone and called Mercedes.

"Adel, is everything okay? Where are you, it's late."

"I need help, Mercedes. Get to my cottage. Come alone. Please."

* * * *

"Did you find out anything?" Hank asked Will as Will stood by his office window and looked out at the evening sky. Adel had left to visit family for a few days, and they weren't happy about not seeing her. It was Monday morning and she should have been back last night. They hadn't heard a word and Hank was concerned. Plus Hank was acting funny. Leo walked in next.

"I haven't heard a word from Adel. What the hell is going on?" Leo asked.

Will turned toward them.

"I don't know how to say this but I think we've been had," Will said and Hank could see the anger in Will's eyes and the disbelief. He instantly felt on edge. He loved his brothers and he would do anything for them.

"What do you mean?" Leo asked, walking toward his desk.

"Look at this," Will said and turned the laptop toward them.

"I just got confirmation from Alex on everything there. She's working against us," Will told them.

Hank took a look and he read the name of the company and the owner and co-owners of Ross Mc K Construction.

"It's her. She's Rick McKinley's daughter. Rick is part owner with Bentley Ross, hence Ross Mc K Construction. Alex pulled her phone records. Adel's been getting numerous calls from this Ross guy's personal cell phone. She probably headed that way this weekend to celebrate pulling one over on us and sealing the deal on the bid for the Morrison project." Will raised his voice and slammed his fist down on the desk.

Hank felt sick. He didn't want to believe this was true. There had to be an explanation.

"She never lied about her name being McKinley," Leo said to them as he pulled out his cell phone.

"Who are you calling?"

"Adel," Leo said.

"No, don't call her and let on that we know she's scamming us. She wants to play this game, fuck with our hearts and pretend that it's only her taking a chance on this relationship, no," Will said and Hank couldn't even respond. He was so hurt. He just couldn't believe that this was real.

"But she tried so hard to help us with the proposal. Her ideas were amazing and right on. Cadence even complimented her organization skills," Leo added.

"Yeah, as she took pictures of our ideas and probably forwarded them to this Ross guy and her father. Why would she need a job when her dad owned this construction business? They're not even hands-on, they're like middle men that subcontract out. It's screwed up, and we fell for her innocent story."

"But, Will, Dad was the one that hired her. He said he knew her family?" Leo pointed out.

"Call him right now. Call Dad and demand an explanation. Something is definitely not adding up here," Hank stated and Will pulled out his cell phone to call their dad, Harold.

* * * *

"You can't hide out forever, Adel, besides, I think you need to see a doctor," Mercedes told her as she got more ice for her lip and cheek."

"I can't go back to the construction company. Bentley will go after Will, Hank, and Leo, maybe even Harold. I can't let him hurt them because of me."

"Are you out of your mind? The man tried to rape you. My God, Adel, you're still bleeding and bruised up. He could have kept you prisoner, hell, killed you. You need to go to the police."

She shook her head and Mercedes slammed her hand down on the table.

"I'm calling Max. I know he's the sheriff but he knows people. I've overheard some of the down-low situations he's helped out in. You need to trust me on this."

Adel closed her eyes. She was in so much pain she ached everywhere.

"Listen, I've already taken the pictures of your injuries. He won't make you go to the hospital and have them do it. Let me call him."

Adel felt the tears roll down her cheeks.

"I don't want Leo, Will, and Hank to know. Please, Mercedes. No one can see me like this."

Mercedes squeezed Adel's hand then pulled out her cell phone.

* * * *

Max was trying to rein in his temper. Beautiful, sweet Adel was a mess, a victim of an attempted rape and assault and she fought her attacker then drove over an hour home with these injuries.

"I took pictures so there's no need to do that, but Adel doesn't want to press charges because of what she explained to you, Max," Mercedes told him.

He was trying to process the entire situation and Adel explained her thoughts and what she wanted to do to ensure that Ferguson construction didn't suffer and that they got the job with the Morrisons.

"Somehow, Adel, I don't think Will, Hank, and Leo are going to give a shit about some fucking job. You're their woman, their responsibility, and they're going to need to see you and know where you are."

"No, Max, I can't let them see me like this. I can't be with them anymore. He'll go after them and destroy their business."

"He made those threats and by telling me I can do what I can to assist you. I've dealt with men like this before, Adel. It's not going to be done exactly by the law, but this son of a bitch isn't playing by the rules."

"I just don't want the construction company to go under because of me."

"What else can you tell me about this guy Bentley Ross?"

Adel explained everything she knew and why she left her family and moved out here to Chance. With each detail, Max could tell she was a fighter and that she really did lose her faith in people and in men. Will, Hank, and Leo would have to really work on gaining Adel's trust and be gentle with her. Letting them know about what happened to her and then telling them she didn't want to see them.

"I think we should call Dr. Anders and ask him to look you over, honey. Just as precaution," Max said and Adel looked at Mercedes.

"It will be okay, honey. I'm worried and I'll feel a lot better if I know that you don't need to be in a hospital."

Max was relieved as she nodded her head. He looked away. The fact that she was beaten and curled up on the couch looking so defeated pissed him off. He was going to help this young woman, and he was going to help his friends Will, Hank, and Leo.

* * * *

"Now calm the hell down. You've got it all wrong," Harold told his sons as he, William, and Ethena met them at the office.

"She lied to us. She's the daughter of one of the owners of Ross Mc K Construction," Will stated.

"I know she is. I'm the one that hired her," Harold told his son.

"You need to explain what's going on. Something isn't right. Adel didn't come back from her trip to see her family," Hank told his dad. Harold felt his chest tighten and he immediately looked at Will and Ethena.

"You need to tell them, Harold. They love her and have a right to know what that monster of a father did to her. Tell them everything. Adel will get over it," Ethena said to Harold and he exhaled then began to explain about Adel's life, how her father sold her out to Bentley Ross and she was engaged to get married.

"Engaged?" Hank asked, looking shocked and suddenly insulted.

"It wasn't her decision. It was forced on her as part of a deal, but Bentley was abusive and he cheated on her. She took off to save herself when her parents wouldn't help. The poor woman went through hell. In fact, she went to see them in hopes of settling things with her dad so she could have some closure and move on with her life with you guys."

"You know this how?" Will asked him. Ethena hugged his arm.

"We talked weeks ago and she mentioned that her mom was hounding her about returning. I told her I didn't think it was a good idea but I understood her reasoning. She's got a big heart and she just wanted to give her dad and mom another chance to show her they really loved her. It was Bentley I was most worried about."

"That guy would be there? He's still involved with the family?" Leo asked.

"Son, they own the company together. He hasn't stopped calling her wanting her back. I think since things took a different turn with the four of you she ignored his calls and didn't respond to him."

"Great, and she couldn't share any of this with us?" Will said.

"Because she was afraid. That man abused her, cheated on her, and used her. Her own father did, too. How the heck can she trust a man, never mind three intense, demanding brothers like the three of you?" their mom asked, raising her voice.

They heard a knock at the door and William opened it.

"Max, what are you doing here?" William asked and Harold caught his eye. He said hello to everyone and gave Ethena a kiss on the cheek.

"I'm glad that you're all here. I thought I was going to have to call for a meeting to speak privately with you."

He looked at the door.

"William, can you close that please?" Max said.

"What's going on?" Hank asked.

"I've got some information, but before you even ask any questions I need you all to hear me out, and respect Adel's wishes for now."

"Adel? What does this have to do with Adel?" Hank asked.

Max looked at Harold and then exhaled as he leaned one hand on his holster and one on his hip.

"Adel's in a bit of trouble, but her main concern is all of you and this company. Seems you have a snitch working in here, and the man he's working for is set out to take down Ferguson Construction."

# Chapter 7

Warner Dawn was asked to do a favor for Mercedes's friend, Adel. Warner had known Will, Leo, and Hank for years and thought of them as good friends. Once he heard about what happened to Adel and the kind of trouble she was in, he arranged to meet with her and go over details of her plan and the sheriff's. As a retired mercenary for the military, he and his brother, Kurt, who shared the same profession, had a lot of connections. Getting some heavy shit on this Bentley character was a piece of cake. Learning about how many women he assaulted over the years, and even about a certain young woman who disappeared after being seen entering a hotel with him, made Warner dig deeper. The right connections and a bit of money went a long way.

Warner sat in Bentley's office waiting for the piece of shit to arrive. He thought about Adel's bruises and battered body and how Bentley tried to rape her and all he kept thinking was that he could eliminate this guy and no one would ever find the body, but that was not what Max wanted done. Adel, despite the damage done emotionally and physically by Bentley and her own parents, had a bigger plan. One that kept her three men and their family safe, their business secure, and one that ensured that Bentley never came near her or her men again.

"Oh, I'm sorry, I wasn't told that someone was waiting for me. Who are you?" Bentley asked Warner. Warner didn't hide his smirk as he saw the black eye and the gash to Bentley's temple that needed stitches and the swollen lip.

"Nice," Warner said and Bentley squinted his eyes.

"Do I know you? Who let you in here?"

"That lovely secretary of yours. Sweet young thing, but not too bright. Left me in here with access to all your computers and files on your desk."

Bentley looked at his desk and then at Warner.

"I think you should leave. I don't even know who you are."

"Well, you're going to get to know me really well. You see, I'm a friend of Adel's."

Bentley lost that intimidated expression and it turned to a pompous one.

"A friend of hers huh? She's nothing but a whore."

Warner clenched his teeth. He so badly wanted to punch this guy's face in. He was a loser, a creep, and a criminal.

"Actually, no, she isn't, but you're a lying piece of shit, and your life is about to change."

"How so?" he asked as he ignored Warner and glanced at the files on his desk, pretending that he didn't care about what Warner wanted. Warner waited and then Bentley opened the file and scanned through the pictures, the documents, and the copies of evidence showing there were probable cause and enough evidence to charge him with assault and attempted rape.

He looked up at Warner with an expression of evilness Warner recognized all too well.

"She's lying and no one will believe her. She's fucking three men. I bet she's fucking you, too."

"Keep looking, asshole. That's just the charges from Adel that she submitted to the police and to her attorney. There's a list of other victims and their written statements accusing you of rape. Oh, and let's not forget the green file. Check it out."

Warner watched as the panicked expression covered Bentley's face and he opened the green file. He lost all coloring and fell back into his chair.

"I hope you enjoyed the good life, the fancy cars, the expensive dinners, and showing off all that hard earned money. Because it will be nothing but a dream where you're going, buddy. Prison is a very bland and humbling experience."

Warner turned around to leave.

"What does she want? I'll do whatever she asks. Just don't hand these over to the police."

"You're nothing but scum. You don't deserve any chances, not after what you did to Adel, what you tried to do to the Ferguson construction company, and what you did to those other women. It's over, Bentley. Adel won and you lost."

Warner headed out of the office, closing the door behind him. As he walked past the secretary he could hear Bentley screaming and raging in his office.

"I'd look for a new job, honey, your boss is taking a very long vacation."

* * * *

Adel got the text message from Warner. He told her it was done. The situation was now over. Bentley was going to jail, she was pressing charges, and so were four other women that Max had gotten to come forward and no longer remain silent about their assaults by Bentley. Adel was relieved as she leaned back on the bed, closed her eyes, and tried to rest. The tears rolled down her cheeks and she let them fall.

"Somebody is in a lot of trouble."

She heard Hank's voice and she saw his face, as well as Will's and Leo's. Their eyes widened and she could tell they were upset at seeing her bruises and her battered body. She rolled to her side and tried covering her face with the pillow.

The bed dipped and Hank was there caressing her hair.

"We've been so worried, baby. Don't shut us out. We're not going to hurt you," Will told her as she felt the bed dip on the other side then right below her feet. She knew they surrounded her and then she felt the gentle caress from Will's hand on her thigh, and Hank's hand moved along her hair and Leo's lips touched her shoulder.

"I didn't want you to see me like this."

"But you're ours and we've been so worried. Plus things are over now. Bentley can't hurt you anymore," Hank told her.

She lowered the pillow.

"I told Max not to tell you anything. I said I wanted to be alone and not have you see me like this."

"Well, things work a little differently in Chance, baby. Everyone knows that a woman's men take the best care of her and that she's their responsibility," Leo said.

Hank pulled the pillow away and held her gaze. He stared into her eyes. The swollen lip and the bruises were definitely making him angry.

"You're a survivor, Adel. You fought hard and you came out on top," he said and then leaned forward and kissed her forehead.

"I don't feel like I'm on top. I feel like I lost what's most important to me."

"Your parents? Why, after all they did to hurt you?" Will asked.

"No, not my parents, you guys. Because of what my father and Bentley did to me, I went there looking for closure so I could open up my heart to each of you, but the truth was, I already opened my heart to you. I didn't need to go there and it nearly cost me the three of you and my life."

"But it didn't. You fought him off and even afterward you organized a pretty high-tech plan to get him back and bring him down. Quite impressive, I must say," Hank told her and she smiled at him. The tears rolled down her cheeks.

"I love the three of you so much, but I didn't want you to get caught in my problems and wind up losing your company because of me."

Hank cupped her good cheek. "Well one thing you need to learn right now is that we're here for you no matter what. It's not your place to decide if we get to help or not. You're our responsibility and we love you. Can't you let us in and let us take care of you?" Hank asked.

"I can try," she whispered.

"Good, so about these bruises, where else are they, and we want to know exactly what went down," Leo told her.

"Just kiss me, Leo, and hold me in your arms and never let me go. Any of you."

"You got it, baby. Always."

\* \* \* \*

Hank and his brothers took turns keeping Adel company as her injuries healed. She wanted to head back to work but they were being overprotective. Even now, as Hank glanced down at her phone buzzing with another text message. Bentley texted numerous times apologizing and asking for forgiveness. Her mother texted, demanding that she stop making up lies and just leave Bentley alone. It made him and his brothers sick with anger and they wouldn't let Adel see this. In fact, Will was getting her a new phone number and new phone.

"Hank?" He heard his name and looked up from her kitchen table. He immediately placed the cell phone into his laptop bag. He didn't want to upset her.

He hurried to get to her.

"Hey, baby, did you need something?" he asked.

"I woke up alone and I got scared."

He caressed her cheek. "I'm right here. I wouldn't leave you alone."

She gave a soft smile.

"I think I need to move around and not be stuck in this house and in my bedroom. I feel stiff and sore and I think it's from doing nothing."

"Honey, your back is all bruised up, your thighs are, too. We just want you to take your time and heal."

She reached out and touched his arm. His cock hardened beneath his jeans. He wanted to make love to her so badly and she wanted that, too, but they were afraid to hurt her, to press against her injuries. She hinted about her inner thighs hurting. The thought that Bentley tried raping her made him see red. It was too much. They needed time to get over it all.

"Are my bruises so ugly that you don't want to touch me or kiss me?" she whispered, and he could see the tears in her eyes. He felt terrible as he caressed her arms and hugged her to his chest.

"No, baby. Not at all. We just don't want to push you to do something you're not ready for. We don't want you to feel any pain."

"But I do feel pain. In here," she said, pulling back and covering her chest where her heart lay with her hand.

He held her gaze and he understood what she meant. She was feeling it, too. The desperate need to be connected on that intimate level.

"Will and Leo are headed over here. We'll wait for them?"

She shook her head.

"I need slow, and they can join us when they come." She squeezed his hand and led him toward her bedroom.

Hank glanced at the front door which he knew was locked. His brothers had a key. Adel had insisted all windows and doors be locked. She was on edge and it made her sleep better having the extra security as well as having him and his brothers there.

When they got into her room the temperature was cool. The AC was on low and the fan rotated at a slow speed. He could hear the soft sound it made, as loud as he heard his own heartbeat.

He looked at Adel as she stood there in a tank top and shorts. He reached for her, caressed her cheek, and then lowered his mouth to hers. When Hank felt her delicate fingers brush through his hair and against his scalp, he had to calm himself down and remember she was bruised. She needed slow and slow he would do.

She ran her hands up under his shirt and as he pulled from her lips she helped him take it off. He reached for her tank top and cupped her breasts underneath them. She wore no bra. It felt so good to cup the large mounds and bring her pleasure. Her eyes closed and she tilted her head back. He looked at the bruises on her cheek bone, her lip, which was almost fully healed, and of course the scratch that disappeared over her breast. Hank lifted her tank top up and over her head and took in a deep breath. Anger filled his heart at the sight of finger marks and of course the scratch.

Adel brought his palm to her lips and kissed the inside of his hand.

"Take away his touch, Hank. Make me feel beautiful and loved."

He lowered to his knees, taking a breast in his palm and then licking the tip of it. "You are beautiful. The most beautiful woman I have even known."

"And loved, by the three of us."

Hank had known his brothers arrived at the sound of the door opening and then closing and locking. They joined him now and immediately Will and Leo removed their shirts and took position next to Adel. They kissed her shoulders on either side. Will brushed her hair from her shoulder and kissed her cheek and whispered into her ear, but Hank could hear him.

"I love you, baby. Stop us if anything hurts."

"It won't hurt. You three would never hurt me. I know that now. I almost lost you."

Hank released her breast and moved down her belly, scattering kisses against her skin. His brothers kissed her, feasted on her breasts, and aroused her body as he pushed her shorts and panties down.

He locked onto the bruises between her thighs and the one toward her groin. He froze. Thoughts that Bentley came that close to raping her made him sick with anger.

She ran her fingers through his hair.

"Please take it away. Help me, Hank. All of you please," she begged and he saw the stray tear escape her eye.

"Get her onto the bed," he told his brothers and Will lifted her up and gently lay her down on the bed. Hank fell between her thighs and caressed her ankles.

He looked at her then at the first set of bruises. He kissed right over them.

"He can never hurt you again. We'll protect you always," he said, and kissed every bruise while his brothers kissed the others along her ribs and then her breasts.

Her pussy creamed and he maneuvered a finger slowly, gently up into her cunt.

"Yesss," she hissed and tilted her head back, widening her thighs, indicating she was okay and needed more.

He leaned down and licked where his finger stroked. She lifted her pelvis. "More, Hank. More. I want all of you. Please," she begged as she reached up and held Will's hair and tilted up to kiss him. Will met her lips and pulled her upward.

"We don't have everything we need," Leo said and Adel released Will's lips and smiled at Leo.

"Top drawer in the brown paper bag."

Leo scrunched his eyes together as Hank pulled his finger from her pussy. He pulled her lower, so her ass and pussy hung over the edge of the bed.

"What do you have in there, Adel?" he asked and she blushed.

"Hot damn, I think someone likes a cock in her ass," Leo said as he held up a large tube of lube.

They all chuckled.

"Well, she's our beautiful princess. We'll give her anything she asks for."

\* \* \* \*

Will swallowed hard he was so filled with emotions right now. It was difficult to say the least, to see their woman's body battered and beaten, but Adel was so strong. She surprised them all the time with her ability to shock them.

Hank lifted her up and hugged her to him. He kissed her deeply as Will removed his pants just like Leo did and then Will laid down on the bed. He stroked his cock as Hank turned Adel around and placed her on top of Will.

The way her eyes lit up as she saw Will lying there penetrated his heart and sealed the deal for him. Adel would be theirs forever.

She lowered down, aligning his cock with her wet cunt and they both closed their eyes and moaned as if it had been forever since their bodies met like this.

She gripped his shoulders and he cupped her cheeks as he thrust up and she counterthrust down. They worked like that together. Moaning, searching for that completion as they anticipated Leo and Hank joining them.

Will caught the tip of her breast with his mouth as Leo joined them, his cock in hand and leaning toward Adel's mouth.

"Are you sure your lips can handle it? They still look a little sore," Leo asked so caringly.

"I want you. I need this, Leo, please don't worry."

Leo caressed her cheek and Will saw the depth of the love his brother had for her in his eyes and his expression.

"If you're sure."

She didn't reply with words but instead with her tongue as she licked along the base of Leo's cock then pulled him partially into her mouth.

Will continued to thrust up into her cunt as he licked her nipple and played with her breasts. Then he felt Adel tighten up and he knew Hank was filling her ass with lube and getting her ready for cock.

"Fuck that feels so snug. He pussy muscles are squeezing my cock so fucking hard," Will said and then he pulled on her nipple with tongue and teeth. Her pussy spasmed with cream as he thrust upward harder.

"I'm coming in, baby. We're going to be one in about two seconds," Hank said and Will could feel the excitement, the intensity of the moment as Leo breached her ass with his cock and all four of them were connected so intimately.

They lay still momentarily. Will's cock in her pussy, Leo's cock in her mouth, and Hank's cock in her ass. She moaned and wiggled between them and Will chuckled.

"Someone is very needy," Leo said, caressing her hair.

"I think we all are," Hank added and then it began. They worked their cocks in and out of her body, knowing with every stroke they claimed her as their woman, part of them forever. Leo came first, growling out her name and shaking as the sounds of Adel swallowing and licking him clean filled the air.

Will's cock hardened and grew bigger and he knew he was there.

"Come with us, Adel. Come now, baby. You're safe with us always. We love you," Hank said to her as he rocked his hips faster, deeper, making her scream. Will and Hank worked together and Will could feel her body tighten just as it felt like he couldn't move inside her cunt it was so tight and full.

"Fuck!" Hank roared.

"Oh God. Oh!" she cried out as she came and Will followed Hank as they roared and thrust a few more times until they released their seed and she collapsed against Will's chest.

Hank eased out of her, kissing her back, her shoulders, and then her ass as Will caressed her skin and moved her damp hair from her cheeks.

"We've got you, baby. This is where you belong."

"I love you guys. I have for a while but was too scared to tell you and to admit it, but I'm not now. I love you so much. I need you. Please, don't ever leave me."

They each caressed her body and told her how much they loved her, too, and that this was only the beginning.

\* \* \* \*

Leo was lying in bed in the dark with his brothers and Adel asleep on her small queen-sized bed. He had a funny feeling in his gut and as he listened to the quietness of the night he thought he heard something.

"Hey, you okay," Hank asked him in a whisper as not to wake Adel and Will. Will still held her against his chest, a small content expression on both their faces.

The sound of glass breaking caught their attention.

They both sat up. Leo placed his finger over his lips and then stepped into his jeans. Hank did the same thing.

"Call Max," Hank said to him. The footsteps got closer and they looked around the room for a weapon of some sort.

"There," Leo whispered next to Hank. Hank saw the thick wooden walking stick. It was one that Carpezi Lynch made and sold at the local fairs. It was solid and would have to do as a weapon.

The door began to creep open and Leo pulled it all the way open, shocking Bentley and catching him off guard. He swung his head toward them and then back to the bed. He looked like some crazy man.

Leo's heart was racing. Bentley, the guy that hurt Adel, the one they saw in the pictures Max showed them, and he was pointing a gun.

"No!" Leo yelled out as he shoved Bentley to the side, giving Hank the opportunity to strike him with the stick.

The gun went off, once, twice as Hank hit Bentley's hands, making the gun fall to the floor. Leo decked him in the nose and then Hank began to strike him.

Leo could hear Adel screaming as the lights illuminated the room. He had to pull Hank off of Bentley as his brother beat the crap out of the man.

"Oh God, Will's shot," Adel screamed and Leo looked up to see the blood on the pillow right above Will's shoulder.

"I'm okay. It's just a scratch," he said, placing his hand over his shoulder.

Leo reached for the cell phone and dialed 911 for an ambulance and asked for the sheriff to be notified about an intruder breaking in.

"Oh my God, Bentley. Is he alive?" she asked as she held onto Leo, placing a shirt over his wound trying to stop the bleeding.

"I fucking hope so," Hank said and as he stood up, his fists were bloody and cracked open.

"It doesn't matter. He's going to jail for a very long time. His lawyers won't be able to post bail for him this time," Leo said then reached over and caressed Adel's tears away from her cheeks.

"It's going to be fine, Adel, but get some clothes on. We don't want anyone seeing this body but us," Hank told her firmly and she hurried off the bed and stepped into her shorts then pulled on a bra and her tank top. She immediately climbed back into bed and went to Will.

"What about you, Will? You're naked."

He smirked.

"Let them come in here and see I was making love to my woman. Our woman, and that should send a clear message that you belong to the Ferguson brothers. Now and forever."

Hank and Leo chuckled but Adel smacked his arm as the sirens blared from outside and the police arrived.

"Everything is going to be just fine now, Adel. Just fine," Hank said. Will looked down at Bentley. Only if this guy was behind bars for good.

# Epilogue

Adel sat on the bench overlooking the construction site. They'd just broken ground a week ago and plans for the new development and community were on their way.

The Morrisons were thrilled with their proposal, plus they had found out about Bentley's criminal actions and what he put Adel through and dismissed his bid entirely, not that it mattered anyway. Bentley was charged with multiple counts of rape, plus four counts of attempted murder and one count of murder. He was going away for life and they would never have to worry about him.

"There you are. We were looking for you," Will said as he, Leo, and Hank joined her by the bench. She stood up and caressed Will's shoulder where he had been shot. He was being quite the character and playing up the whole bullet wound scar and how cool it was. She got mad at him a few times for saying it was cool, but she had to admit the scar was sexy.

"Are you ready to head to lunch?" Hank asked, taking her hand and pulling it to his lips, kissing the knuckles."

"Sure. I just like sitting here and imagining what this place will look like in three years. There's a lot of work ahead of us."

"There sure is but we're in this together," Leo told her and she smiled. They had insisted on offering her part ownership in Fergusons construction. Their dad Harold decided to sell her half his shares in the company, making her a partner.

"Oh, we got something for you, to make this whole partnership thing official," Leo told her and then pulled out a small black velvet box.

"What is it? You didn't have to give me anything," she said.

Will caressed her cheek and then slid his hand onto her shoulder, squeezing it. She placed her hand over his hand and smiled. "We wanted to."

"We hope you like it. Hank said you had something similar but it wasn't quite right for you," Leo said and she opened up the box.

Her eyes filled with tears and she covered her mouth to hide the joy, the emotions that filled her. It was a small gold heart covered in diamonds. Real gold and real diamonds, like the fake one she had and wore the night of the dinner, except this was the real thing. It sparkled in the sunlight. The diamonds surrounding the gold heart were gorgeous. She looked up at Hank.

"How did you know?" she asked and then Hank reached out and touched the fake gold heart and diamond pendant she wore right now. She had forgotten she had it on. It was her only piece of jewelry.

Leo reached around and unclipped it from her neck.

Will put on the real one.

"This is the kind of jewelry you deserve. Ones made for a princess, a beautiful, loving woman who has made the three of us happy and complete," Hank said then kissed her.

She hugged him tight and held onto him as she looked at Will and Leo, who smiled wide and caressed her back.

She took a chance, a dare to forgive and to open up her heart and love again because of these three men. They were a part of her now and always would be. She never knew what love really was until she met Will, Hank, and Leo. Now that she found love, and felt its power and abilities, she would never let them go.

# THE END

**WWW.DIXIELYNNDWYER.COM**

# ABOUT THE AUTHOR

People seem to be more interested in my name than where I get my ideas for my stories from. So I might as well share the story behind my name with all my readers.

My momma was born and raised in New Orleans. At the age of twenty, she met and fell in love with an Irishman named Patrick Riley Dwyer. Needless to say, the family was a bit taken aback by this as they hoped she would marry a family friend. It was a modern day arranged marriage kind of thing and my momma downright refused.

Being that my momma's families were descendants of the original English speaking Southerners, they wanted the family blood line to stay pure. They were wealthy and my father's family was poor.

Despite attempts by my grandpapa to make Patrick leave and destroy the love between them, my parents married. They recently celebrated their sixtieth wedding anniversary.

I am one of six children born to Patrick and Lynn Dwyer. I am a combination of both Irish and a true Southern belle. With a name like Dixie Lynn Dwyer it's no wonder why people are curious about my name.

Just as my parents had a love story of their own, I grew up intrigued by the lifestyles of others. My imagination as well as my need to stray from the straight and narrow made me into the woman I am today.

Enjoy *Dare to Forgive* and allow your imagination to soar freely.

*For all titles by Dixie Lynn Dwyer, please visit*
www.bookstrand.com/dixie-lynn-dwyer

**Siren Publishing, Inc.**
www.SirenPublishing.com

Lightning Source UK Ltd.
Milton Keynes UK
UKOW06f1835261115

263616UK00015B/416/P